Canada Council for the Arts | Conseil des arts du Canada

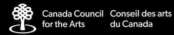

We acknowledge the support of the Canada Council for the Arts.
Nous remercions le Conseil des arts du Canada de son soutien.

HighWater Press gratefully acknowledges the financial support of the Province of Manitoba through the Department of Sport, Culture and Heritage and the Manitoba Book Publishing Tax Credit, and the Government of Canada through the Canada Book Fund (CBF), for our publishing activities.

HighWater Press is an imprint of Portage & Main Press.
Printed and bound in Canada by Friesens
Design by Jennifer Lum
Cover Art by Scott B. Henderson

Library and Archives Canada Cataloguing in Publication
Title: Breakdown / David A. Robertson, Scott B. Henderson, Donovan Yaciuk.
Names: Robertson, David, 1977- author. | Henderson, Scott B., illustrator. | Yaciuk, Donovan, 1975- illustrator.
Description: Series statement: The Reckoner rises ; 1
Identifiers: Canadiana (print) 20200198548 Canadiana (ebook) 20200198564 | ISBN 9781553798903 (softcover) | ISBN 9781553798910 (EPUB) | ISBN 9781553798927 (PDF)
Subjects: LCGFT: Graphic novels.
Classification: LCC PN6733.R63 B74 2020 | DDC j741.5/971—dc23

23 22 21 20   1 2 3 4 5

Also issued in electronic format:
ISBN: 978-1-55379-891-0 (ePUB)
ISBN: 978-1-55379-892-7 (PDF)

HIGHWATER PRESS
www.highwaterpress.com
Winnipeg, Manitoba
Treaty 1 Territory and homeland of the Métis Nation

THE RECKONER RISES

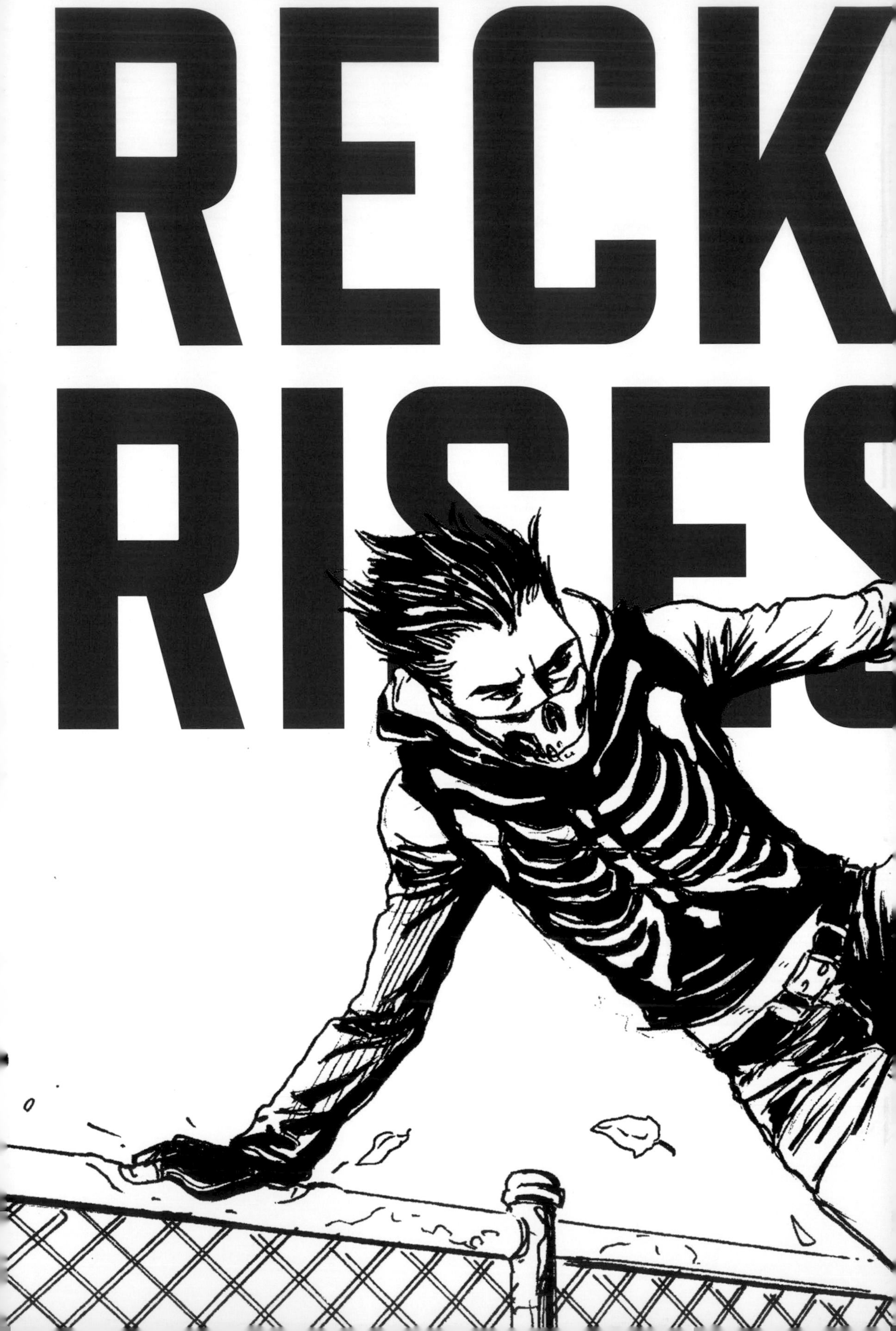
RECK
RISES

ONER

VOLUME 1

BREAKDOWN

STORY | **David A. Robertson**

ART | **Scott B. Henderson**

COLOURS | **Donovan Yaciuk**

LETTERS | **Andrew Thomas**

HIGHWATER PRESS

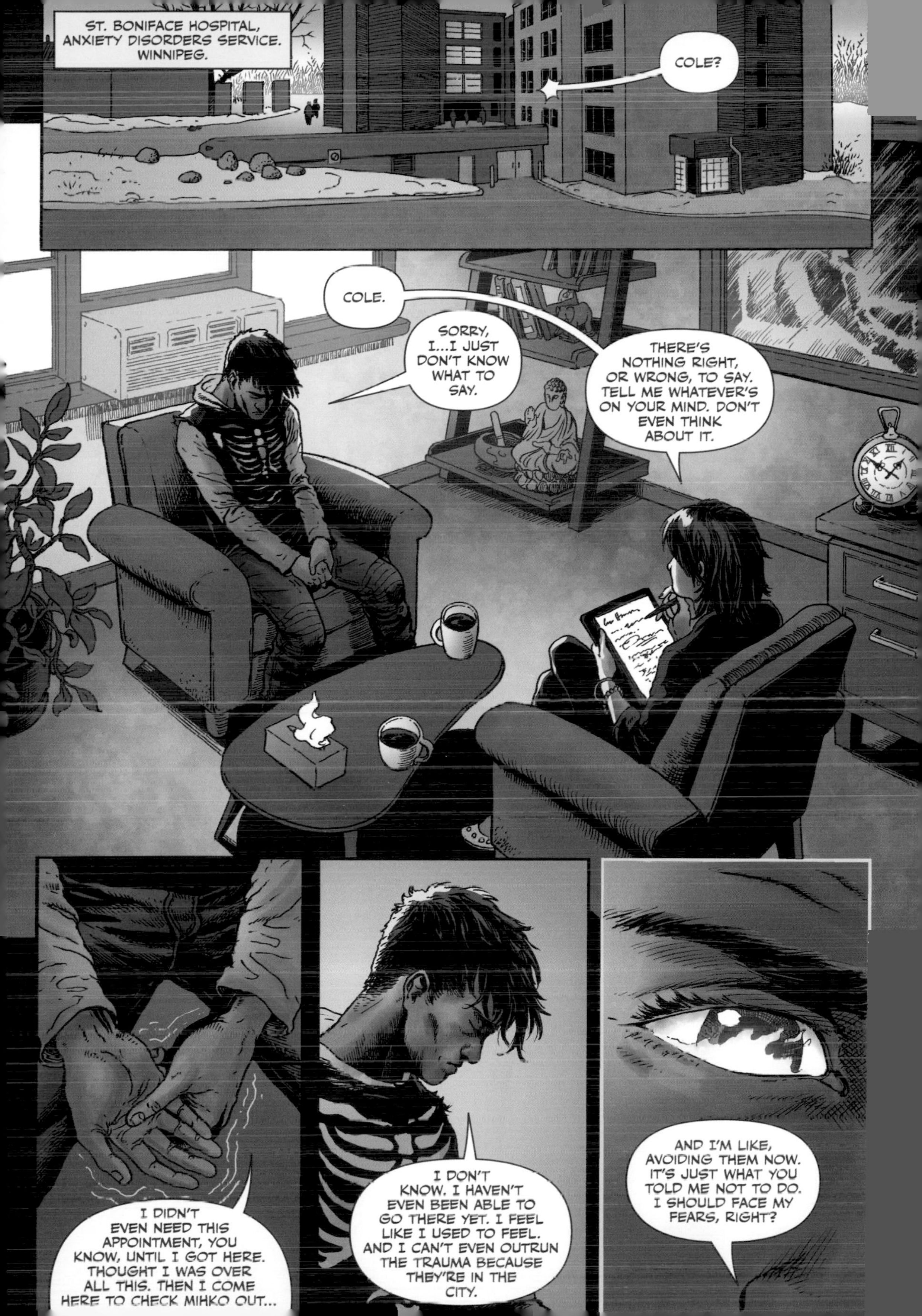

ST. BONIFACE HOSPITAL, ANXIETY DISORDERS SERVICE. WINNIPEG.
COLE?
COLE.
SORRY, I...I JUST DON'T KNOW WHAT TO SAY.
THERE'S NOTHING RIGHT, OR WRONG, TO SAY. TELL ME WHATEVER'S ON YOUR MIND. DON'T EVEN THINK ABOUT IT.
I DIDN'T EVEN NEED THIS APPOINTMENT, YOU KNOW, UNTIL I GOT HERE. THOUGHT I WAS OVER ALL THIS. THEN I COME HERE TO CHECK MIHKO OUT...
I DON'T KNOW. I HAVEN'T EVEN BEEN ABLE TO GO THERE YET. I FEEL LIKE I USED TO FEEL. AND I CAN'T EVEN OUTRUN THE TRAUMA BECAUSE THEY'RE IN THE CITY.
AND I'M LIKE, AVOIDING THEM NOW. IT'S JUST WHAT YOU TOLD ME NOT TO DO. I SHOULD FACE MY FEARS, RIGHT?

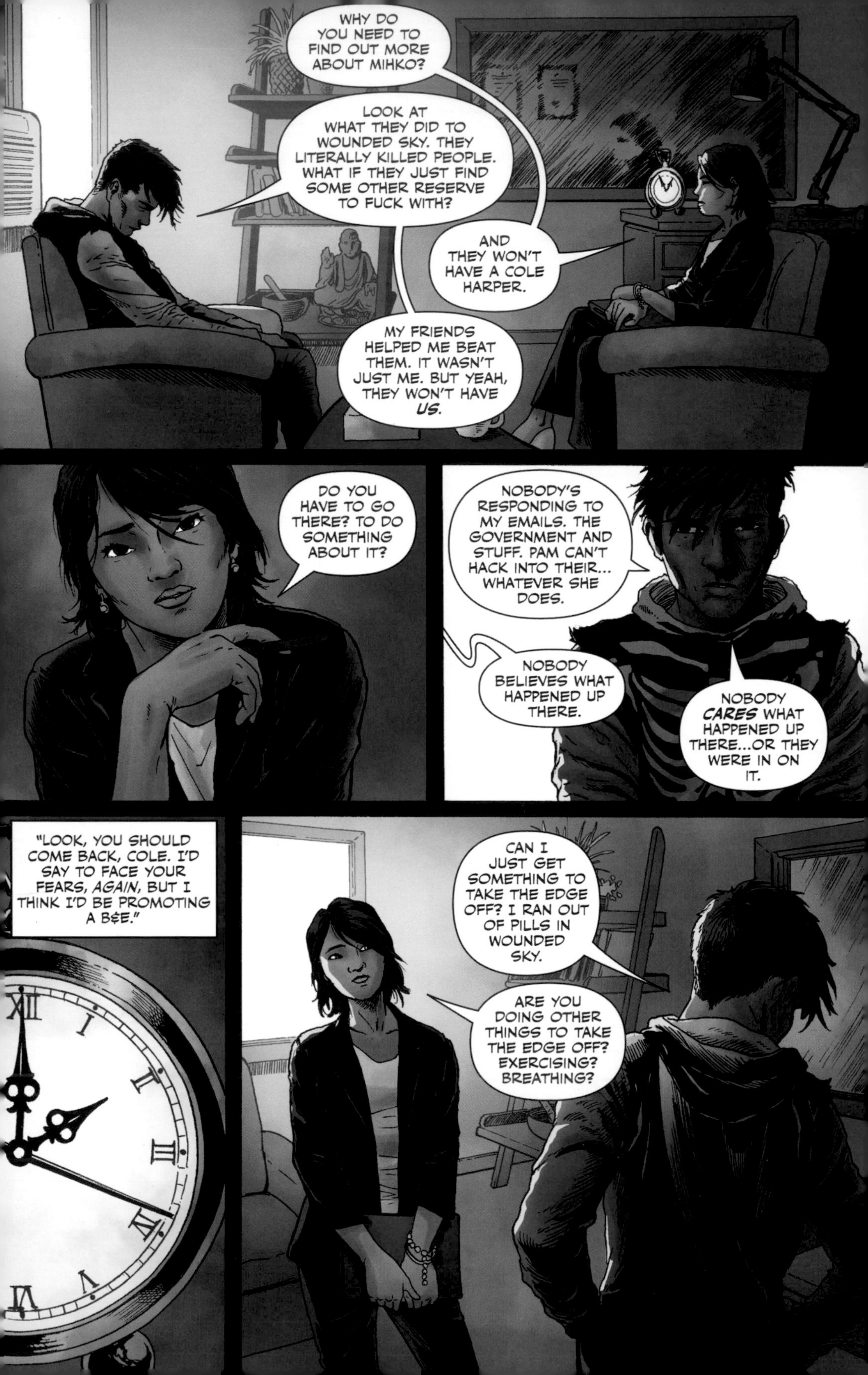
WHY DO YOU NEED TO FIND OUT MORE ABOUT MIHKO?
LOOK AT WHAT THEY DID TO WOUNDED SKY. THEY LITERALLY KILLED PEOPLE. WHAT IF THEY JUST FIND SOME OTHER RESERVE TO FUCK WITH?
AND THEY WON'T HAVE A COLE HARPER.
MY FRIENDS HELPED ME BEAT THEM. IT WASN'T JUST ME. BUT YEAH, THEY WON'T HAVE US.
DO YOU HAVE TO GO THERE? TO DO SOMETHING ABOUT IT?
NOBODY'S RESPONDING TO MY EMAILS. THE GOVERNMENT AND STUFF. PAM CAN'T HACK INTO THEIR... WHATEVER SHE DOES.
NOBODY BELIEVES WHAT HAPPENED UP THERE.
NOBODY CARES WHAT HAPPENED UP THERE...OR THEY WERE IN ON IT.
"LOOK, YOU SHOULD COME BACK, COLE. I'D SAY TO FACE YOUR FEARS, AGAIN, BUT I THINK I'D BE PROMOTING A B&E."
CAN I JUST GET SOMETHING TO TAKE THE EDGE OFF? I RAN OUT OF PILLS IN WOUNDED SKY.
ARE YOU DOING OTHER THINGS TO TAKE THE EDGE OFF? EXERCISING? BREATHING?

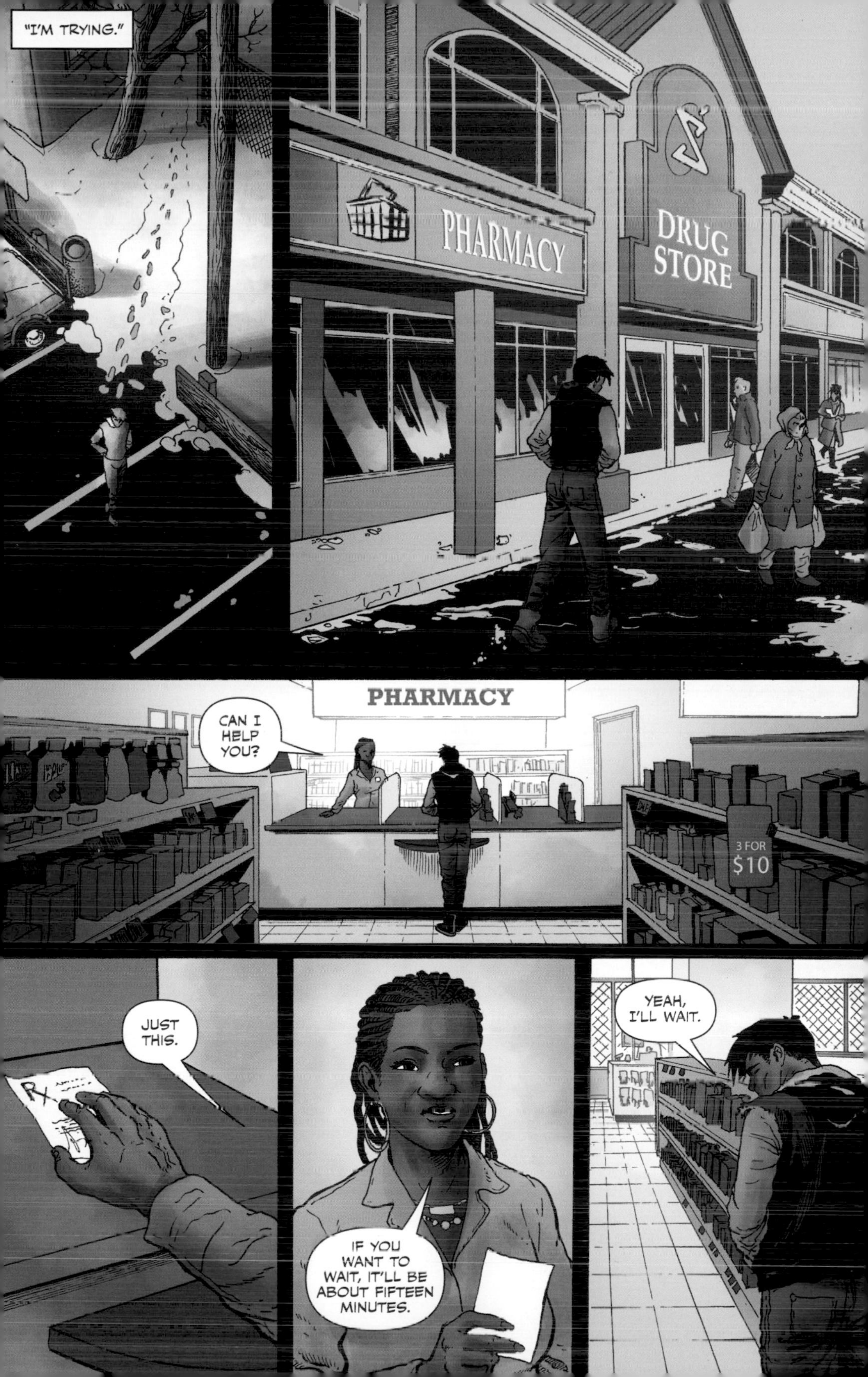
"I'M TRYING."
PHARMACY
DRUG STORE
PHARMACY
CAN I HELP YOU?
3 FOR $10
JUST THIS.
IF YOU WANT TO WAIT, IT'LL BE ABOUT FIFTEEN MINUTES.
YEAH, I'LL WAIT.

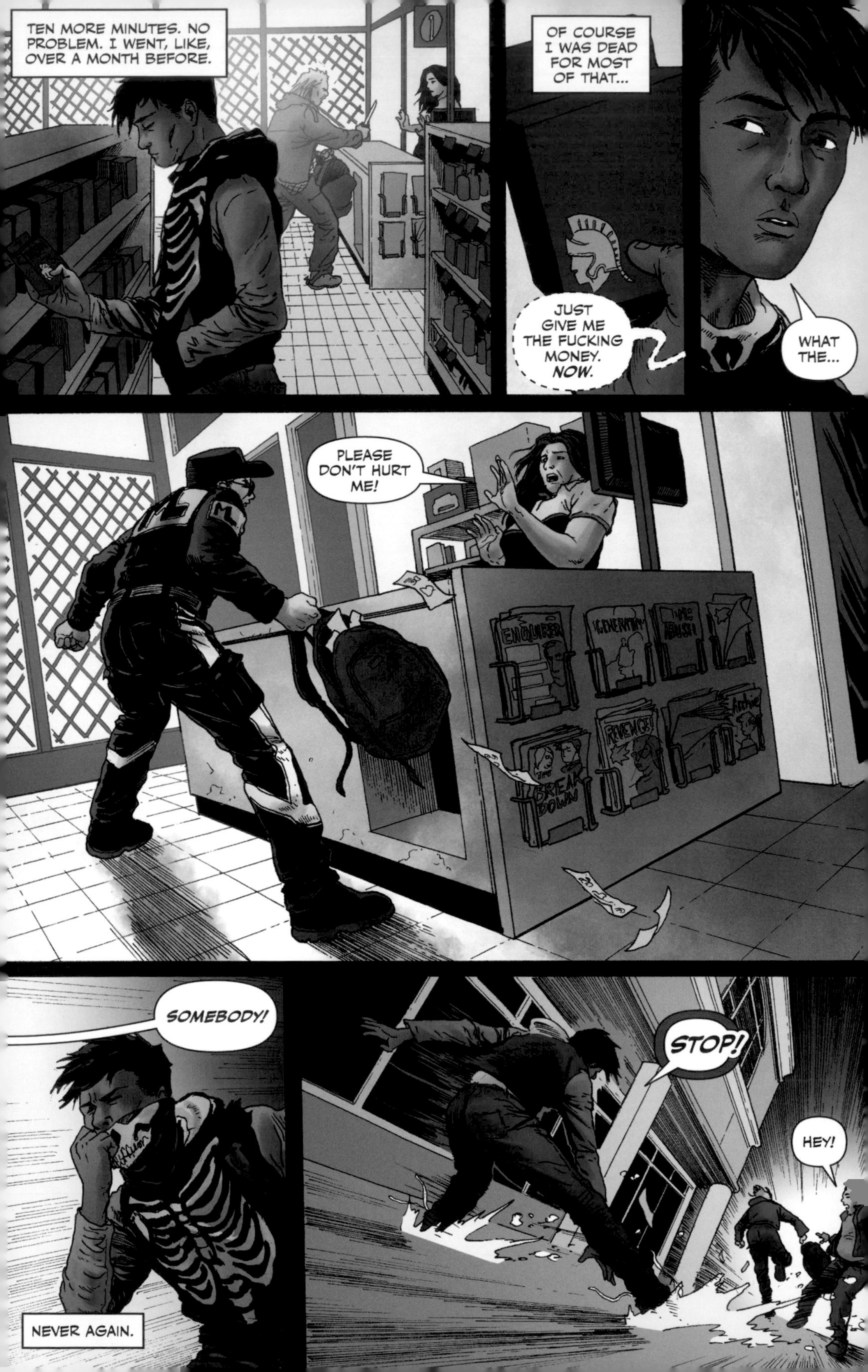
TEN MORE MINUTES. NO PROBLEM. I WENT, LIKE, OVER A MONTH BEFORE.
OF COURSE I WAS DEAD FOR MOST OF THAT...
JUST GIVE ME THE FUCKING MONEY. NOW.
WHAT THE...
PLEASE DON'T HURT ME!
ENQUIRER
GENERATION
REVENGE!
BREAK DOWN
Archie
SOMEBODY!
NEVER AGAIN.
STOP!
HEY!

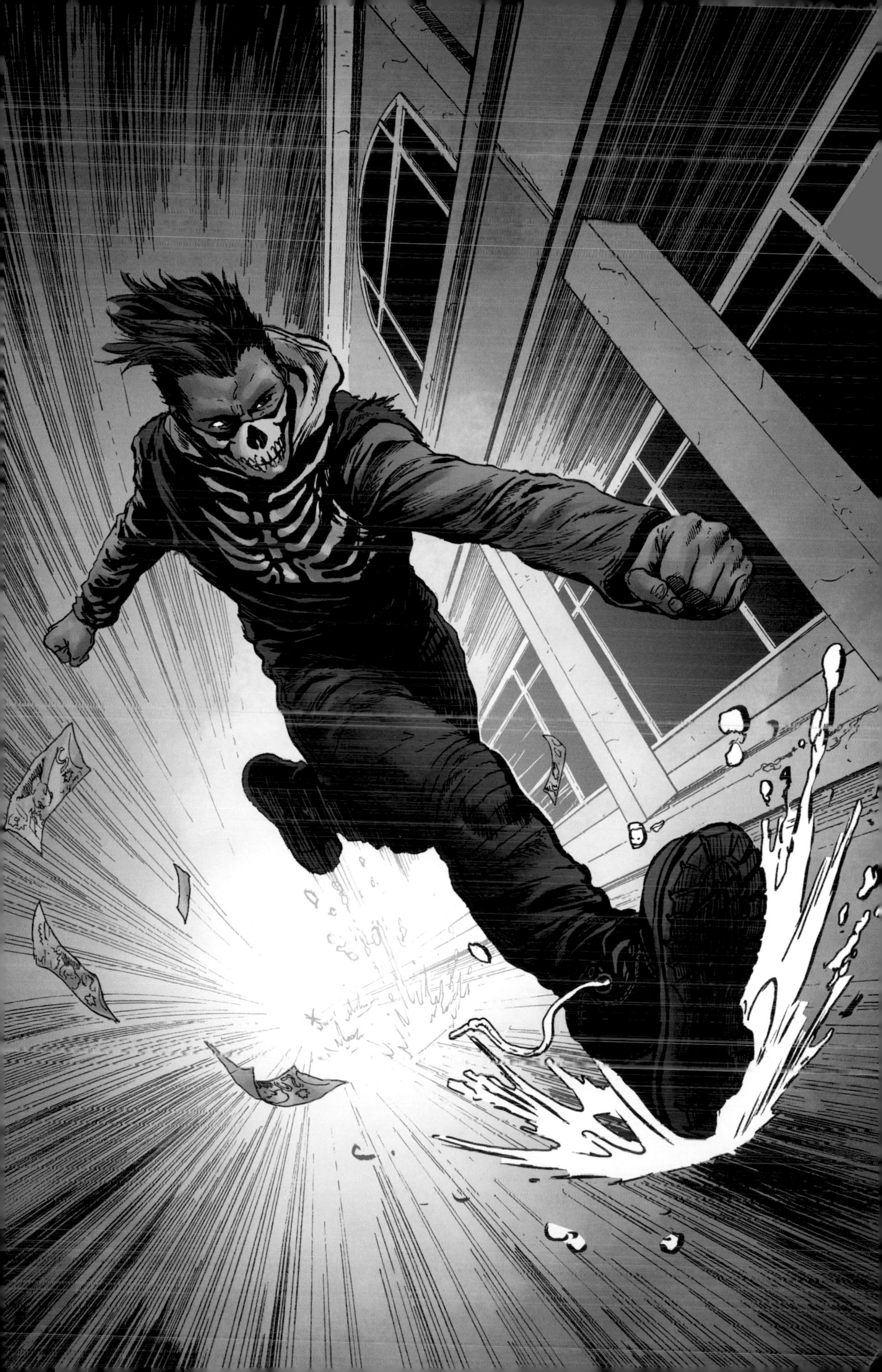

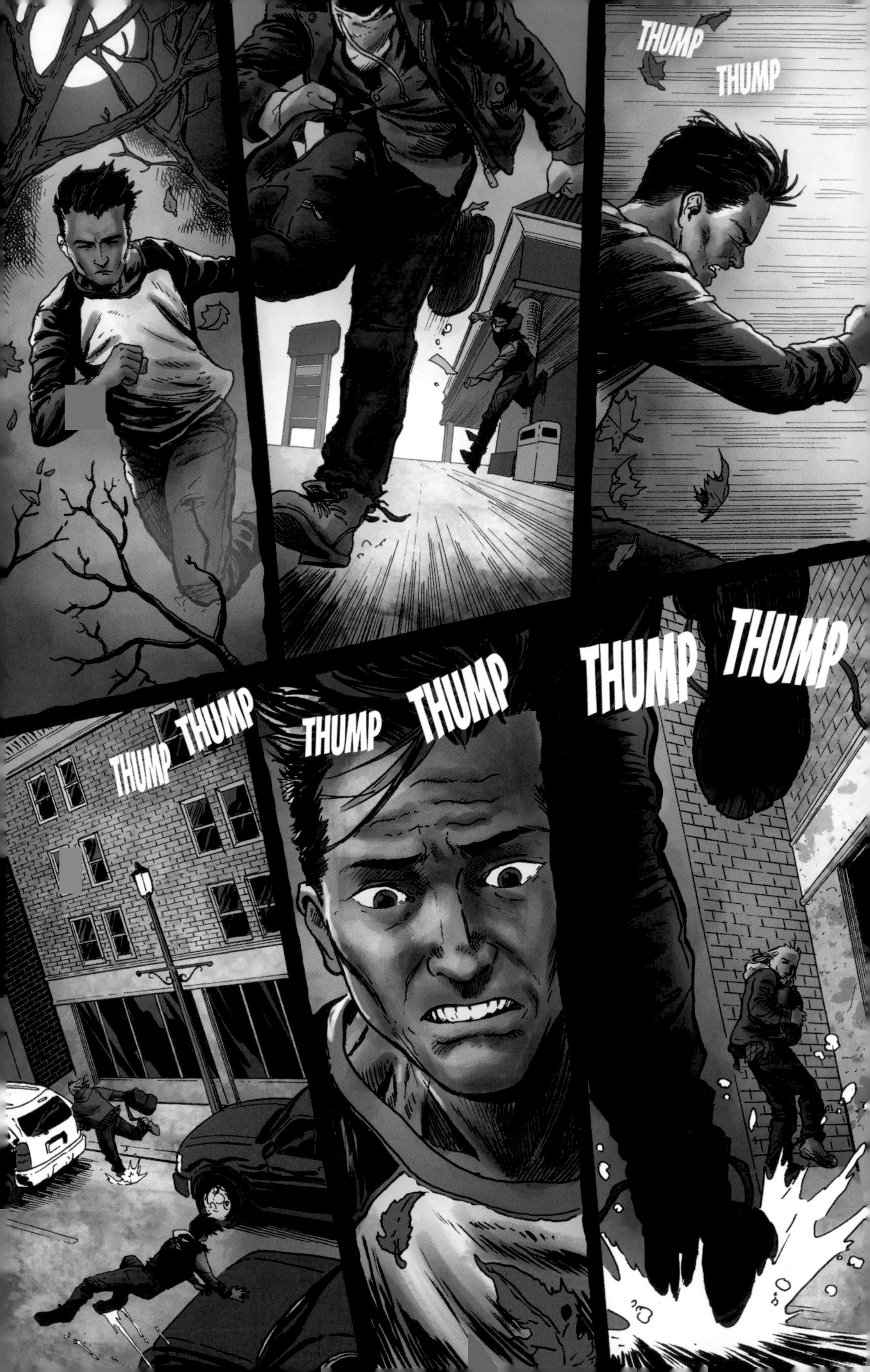
THUMP
THUMP
THUMP THUMP
THUMP THUMP
THUMP THUMP

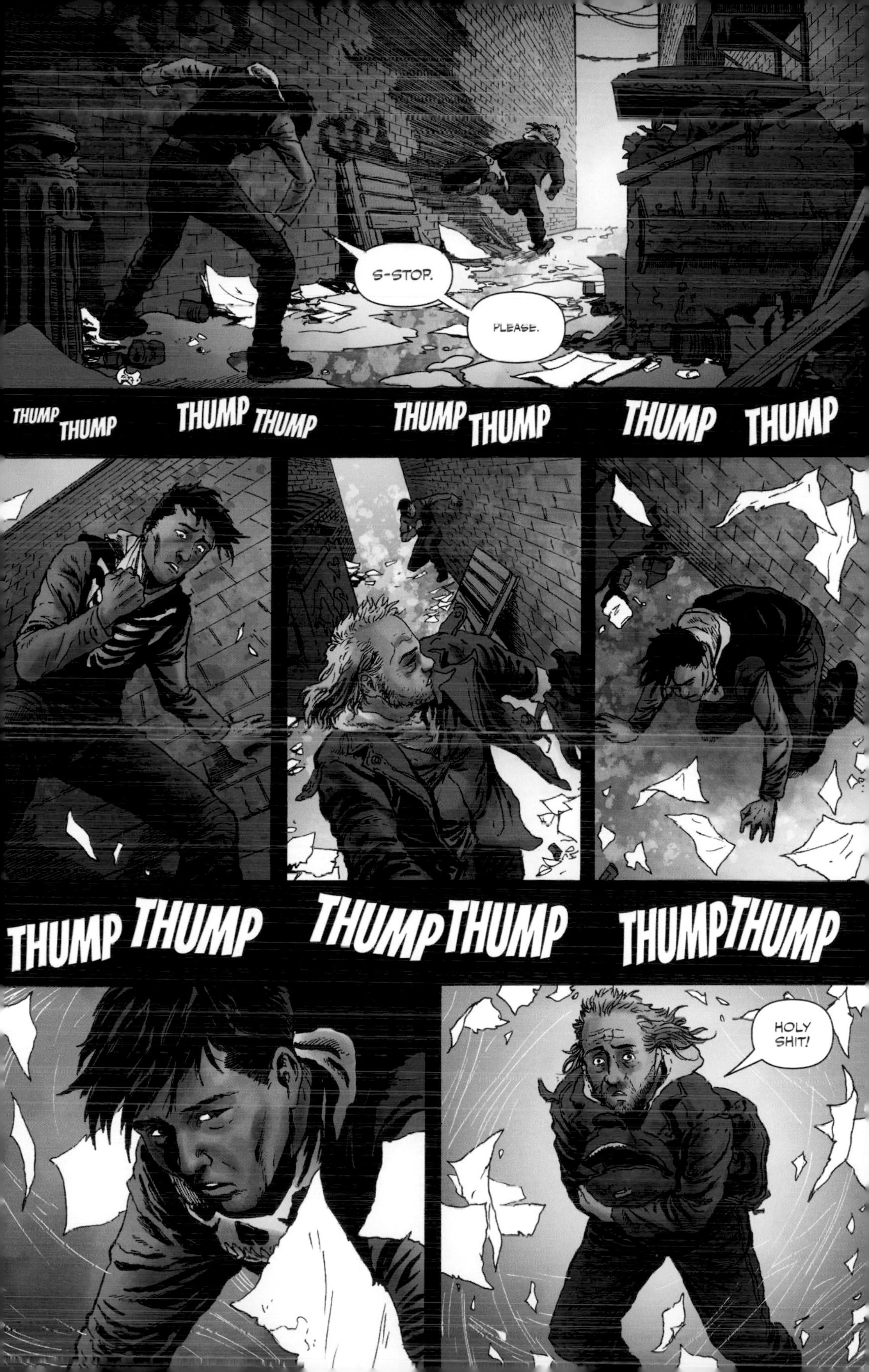
S-STOP.
PLEASE.
THUMP THUMP THUMP THUMP THUMP THUMP THUMP THUMP
THUMP THUMP THUMP THUMP THUMP THUMP
HOLY SHIT!

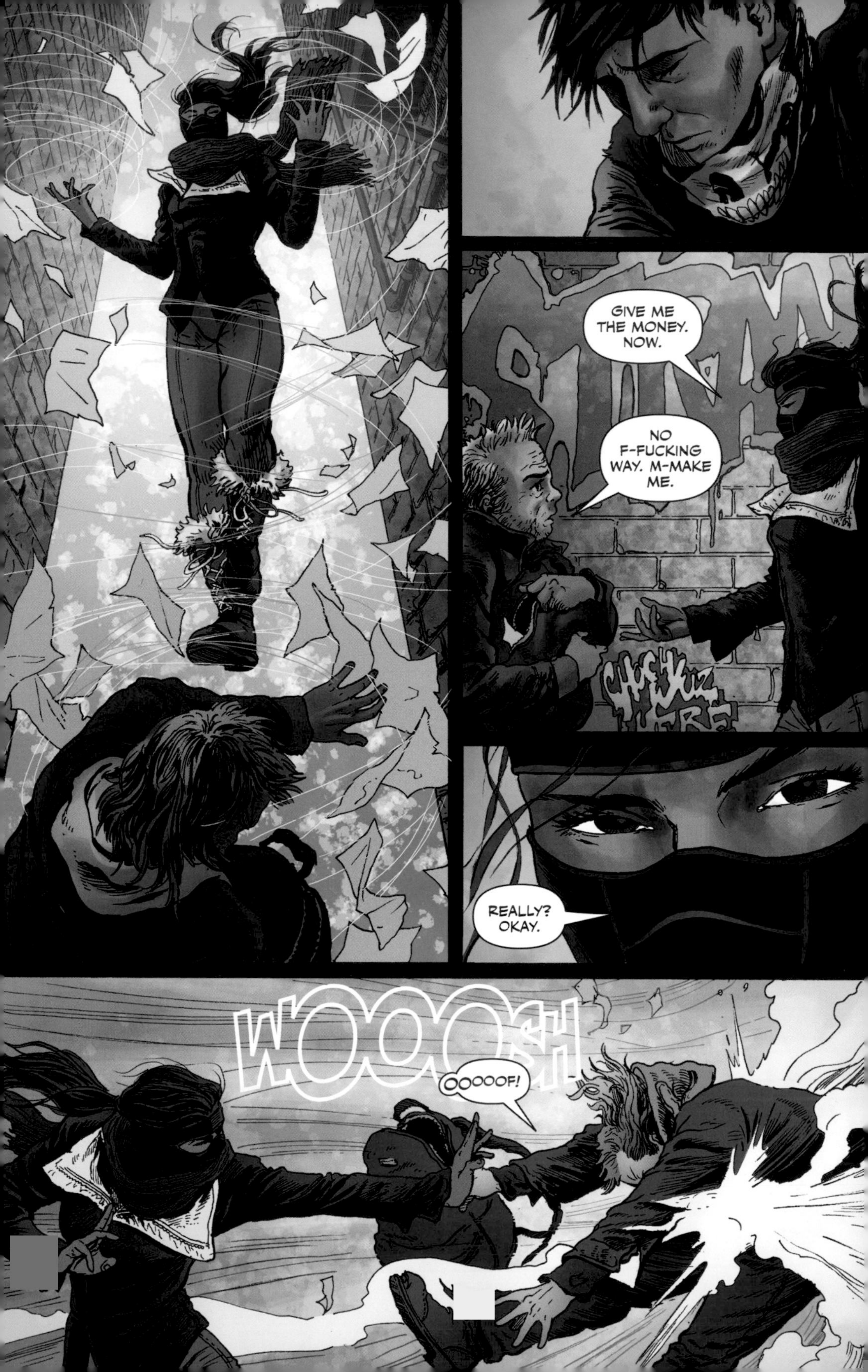
GIVE ME THE MONEY. NOW.
NO F-FUCKING WAY. M-MAKE ME.
REALLY? OKAY.
WOOOOSH
OOOOOF!

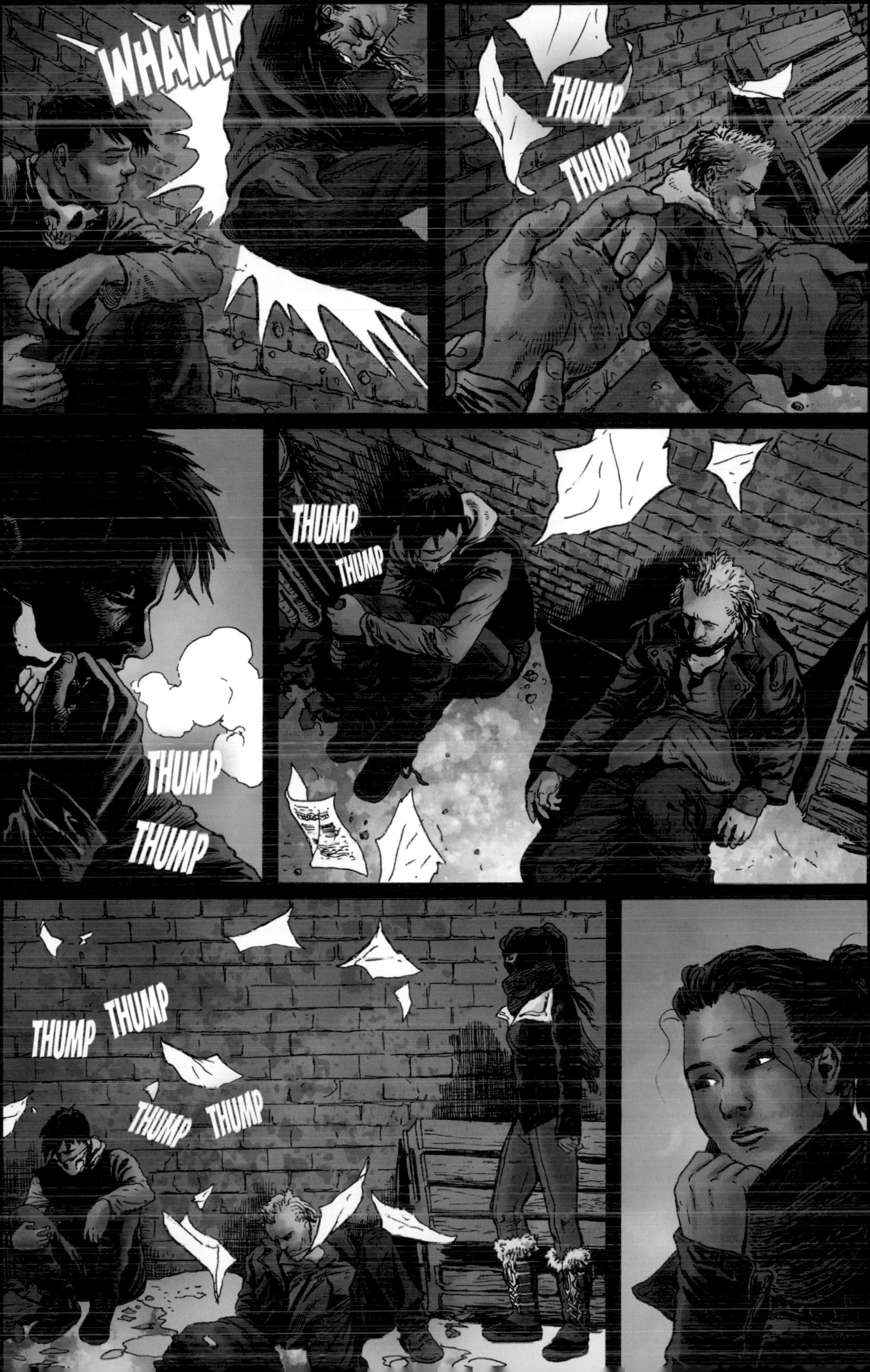
WHAM!
THUMP
THUMP
THUMP
THUMP
THUMP
THUMP
THUMP
THUMP
THUMP
THUMP

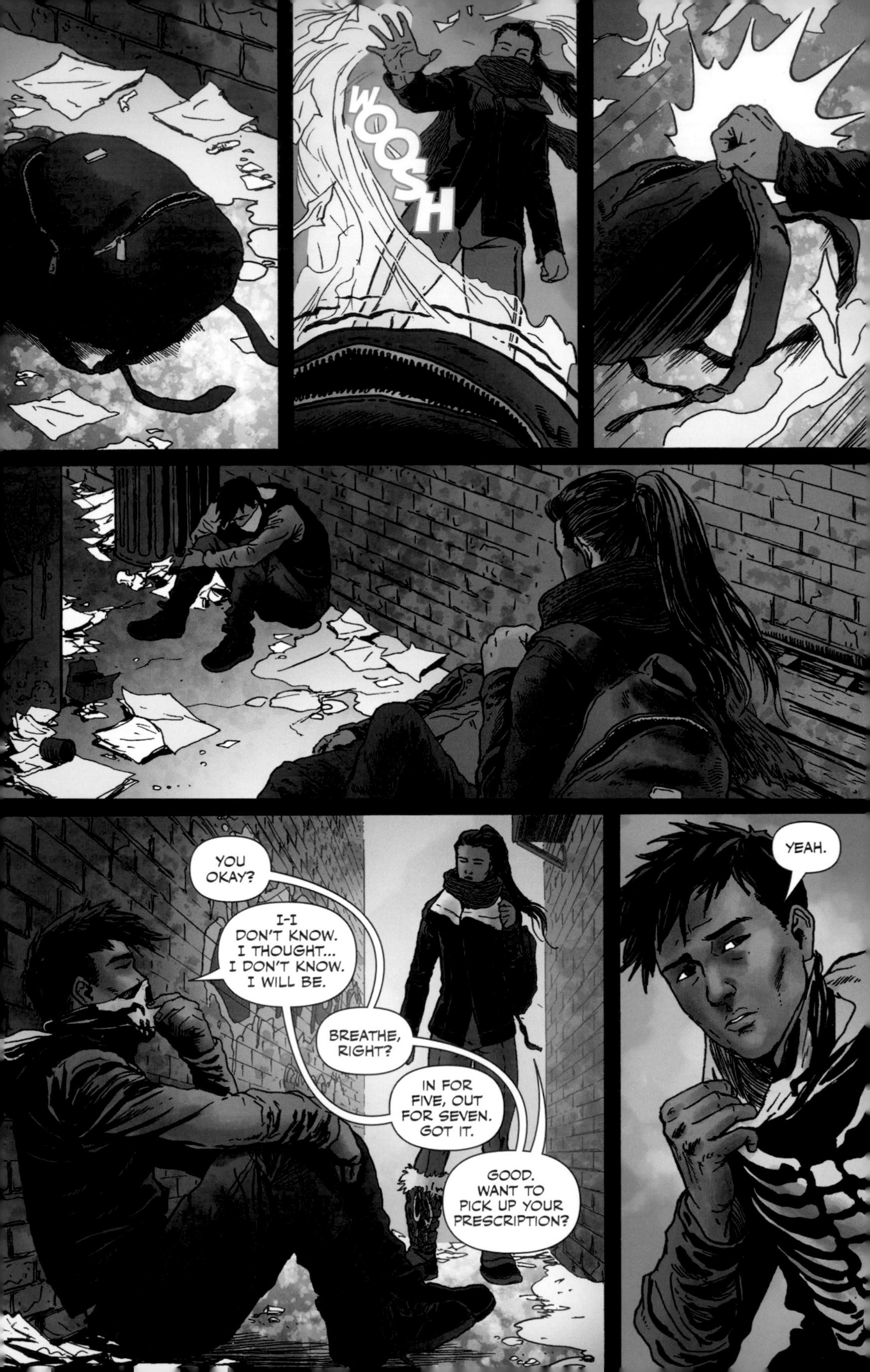
WOOSH
YOU OKAY?
I-I DON'T KNOW. I THOUGHT... I DON'T KNOW. I WILL BE.
BREATHE, RIGHT?
IN FOR FIVE, OUT FOR SEVEN. GOT IT.
GOOD. WANT TO PICK UP YOUR PRESCRIPTION?
YEAH.

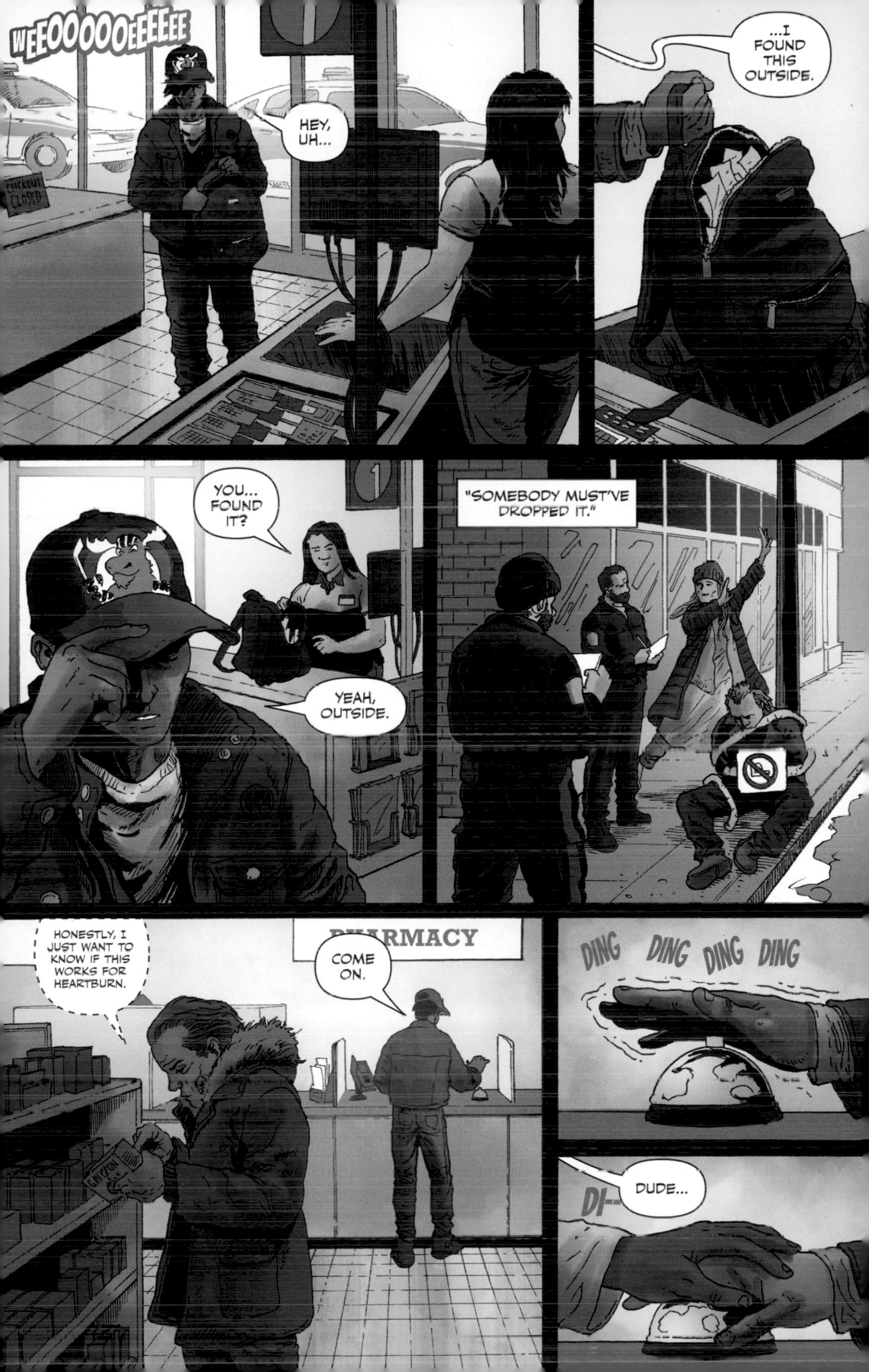
WEEOOOOOOEEEEEE
CHECKOUT CLOSED
HEY, UH...
...I FOUND THIS OUTSIDE.
YOU... FOUND IT?
YEAH, OUTSIDE.
"SOMEBODY MUST'VE DROPPED IT."
HONESTLY, I JUST WANT TO KNOW IF THIS WORKS FOR HEARTBURN.
PHARMACY
COME ON.
DING DING DING DING
DI--
DUDE...

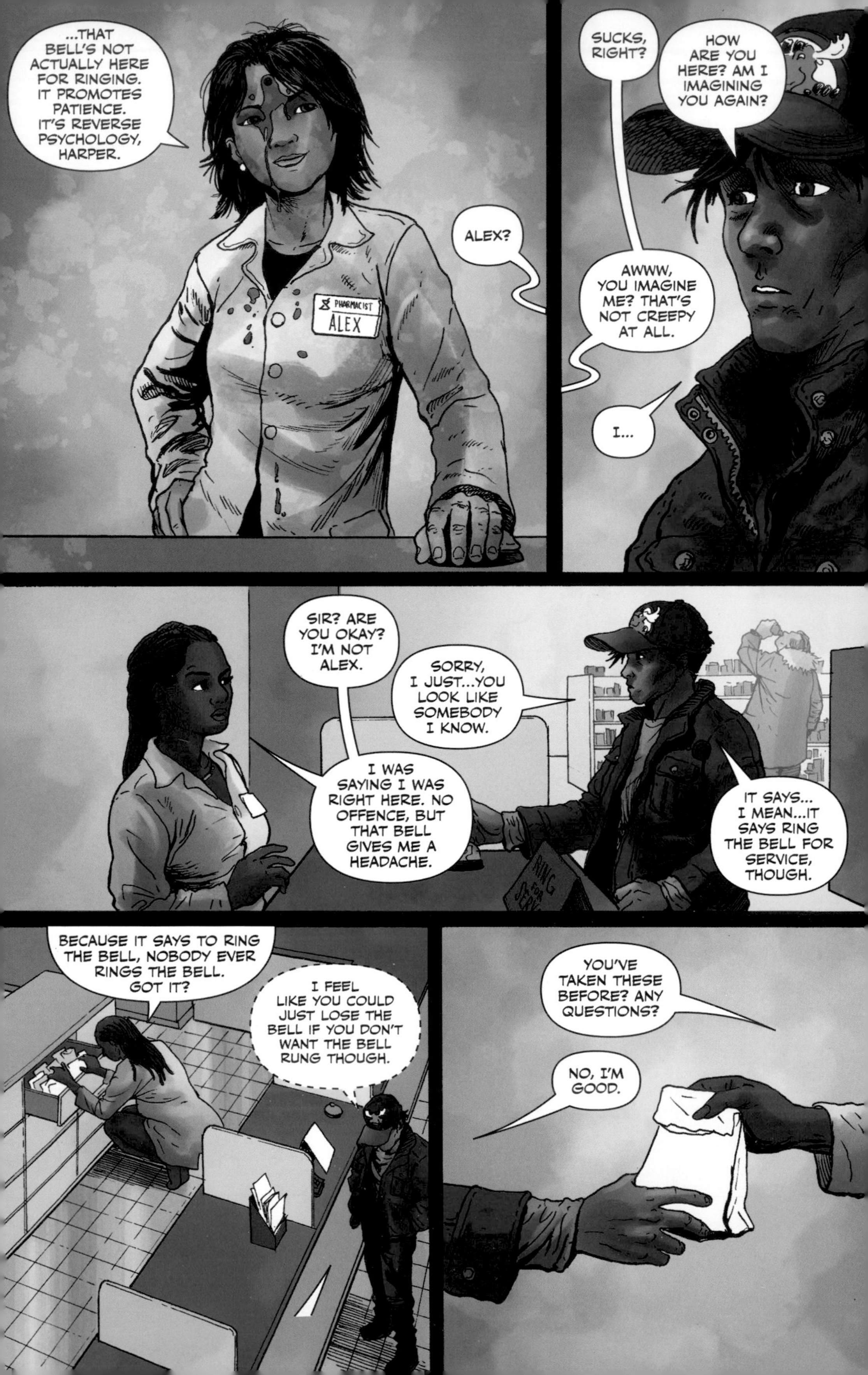
...THAT BELL'S NOT ACTUALLY HERE FOR RINGING. IT PROMOTES PATIENCE. IT'S REVERSE PSYCHOLOGY, HARPER.
PHARMACIST
ALEX
ALEX?
SUCKS, RIGHT?
HOW ARE YOU HERE? AM I IMAGINING YOU AGAIN?
AWWW, YOU IMAGINE ME? THAT'S NOT CREEPY AT ALL.
I...
SIR? ARE YOU OKAY? I'M NOT ALEX.
SORRY, I JUST...YOU LOOK LIKE SOMEBODY I KNOW.
I WAS SAYING I WAS RIGHT HERE. NO OFFENCE, BUT THAT BELL GIVES ME A HEADACHE.
IT SAYS... I MEAN...IT SAYS RING THE BELL FOR SERVICE, THOUGH.
BECAUSE IT SAYS TO RING THE BELL, NOBODY EVER RINGS THE BELL. GOT IT?
I FEEL LIKE YOU COULD JUST LOSE THE BELL IF YOU DON'T WANT THE BELL RUNG THOUGH.
YOU'VE TAKEN THESE BEFORE? ANY QUESTIONS?
NO, I'M GOOD.

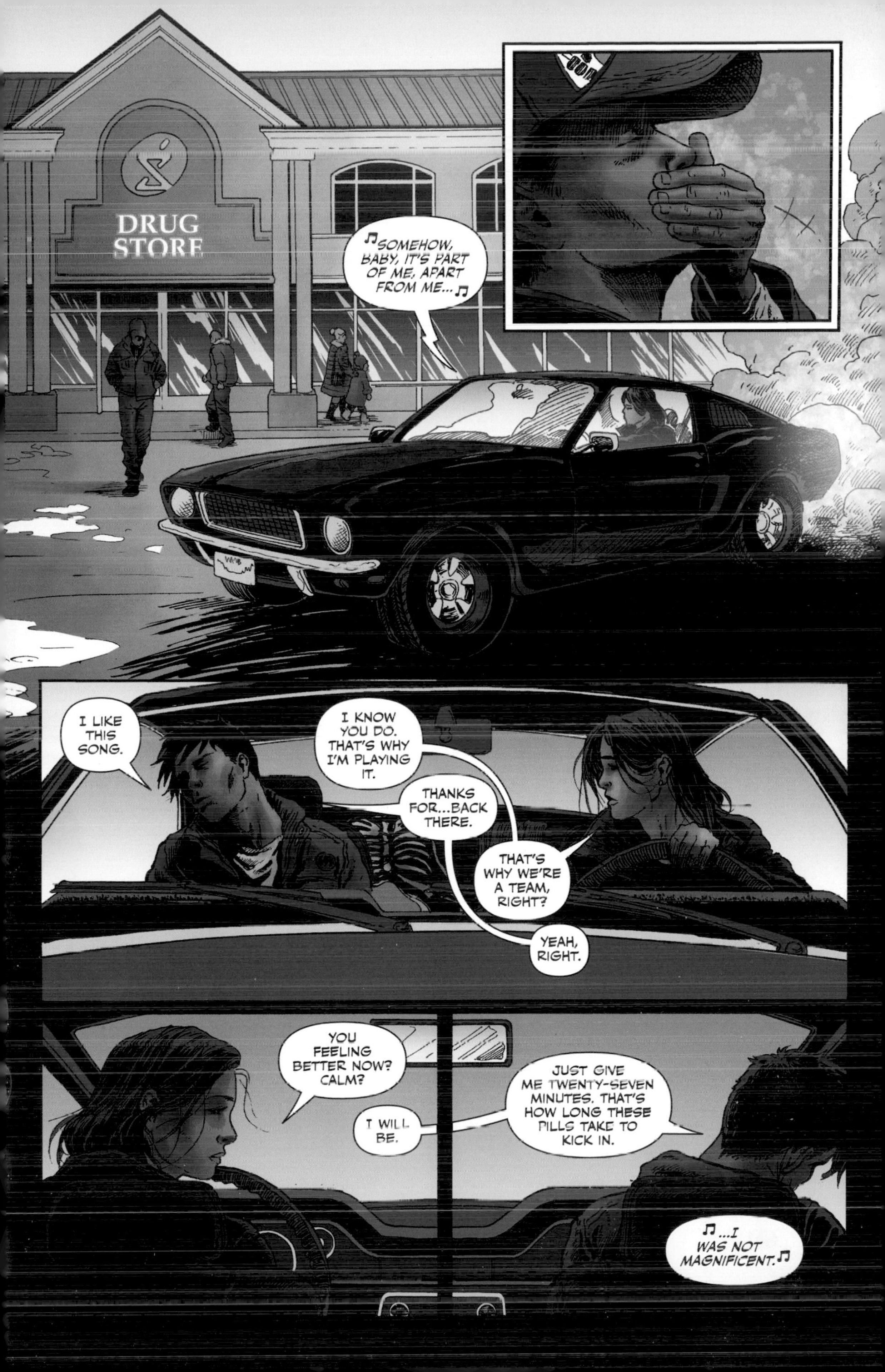
DRUG STORE
♫SOMEHOW, BABY, IT'S PART OF ME, APART FROM ME...♫
I LIKE THIS SONG.
I KNOW YOU DO. THAT'S WHY I'M PLAYING IT.
THANKS FOR...BACK THERE.
THAT'S WHY WE'RE A TEAM, RIGHT?
YEAH, RIGHT.
YOU FEELING BETTER NOW? CALM?
I WILL BE.
JUST GIVE ME TWENTY-SEVEN MINUTES. THAT'S HOW LONG THESE PILLS TAKE TO KICK IN.
♫...I WAS NOT MAGNIFICENT.♫

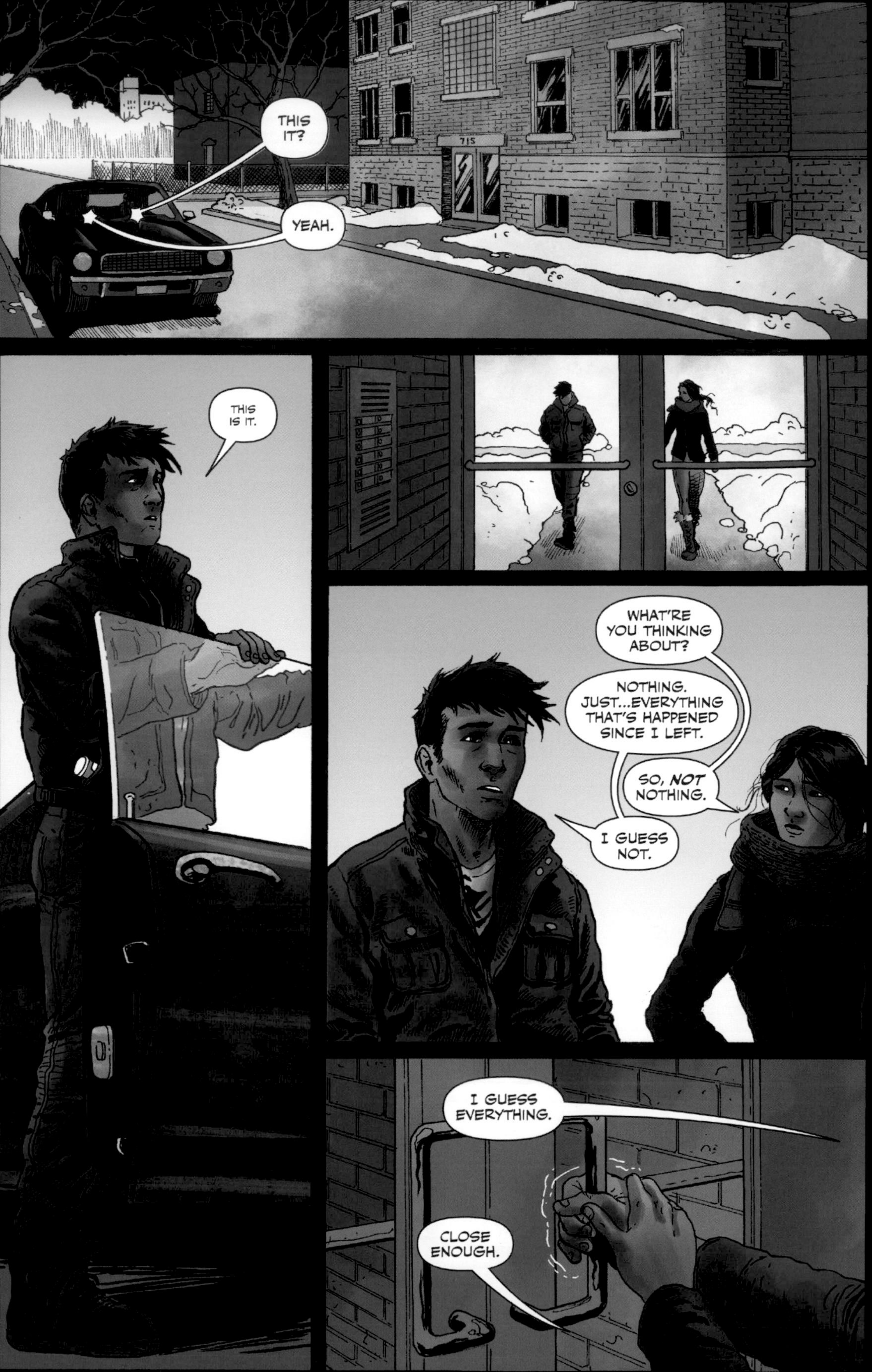
THIS IT?
YEAH.
715
THIS IS IT.
WHAT'RE YOU THINKING ABOUT?
NOTHING. JUST...EVERYTHING THAT'S HAPPENED SINCE I LEFT.
SO, *NOT* NOTHING.
I GUESS NOT.
I GUESS EVERYTHING.
CLOSE ENOUGH.

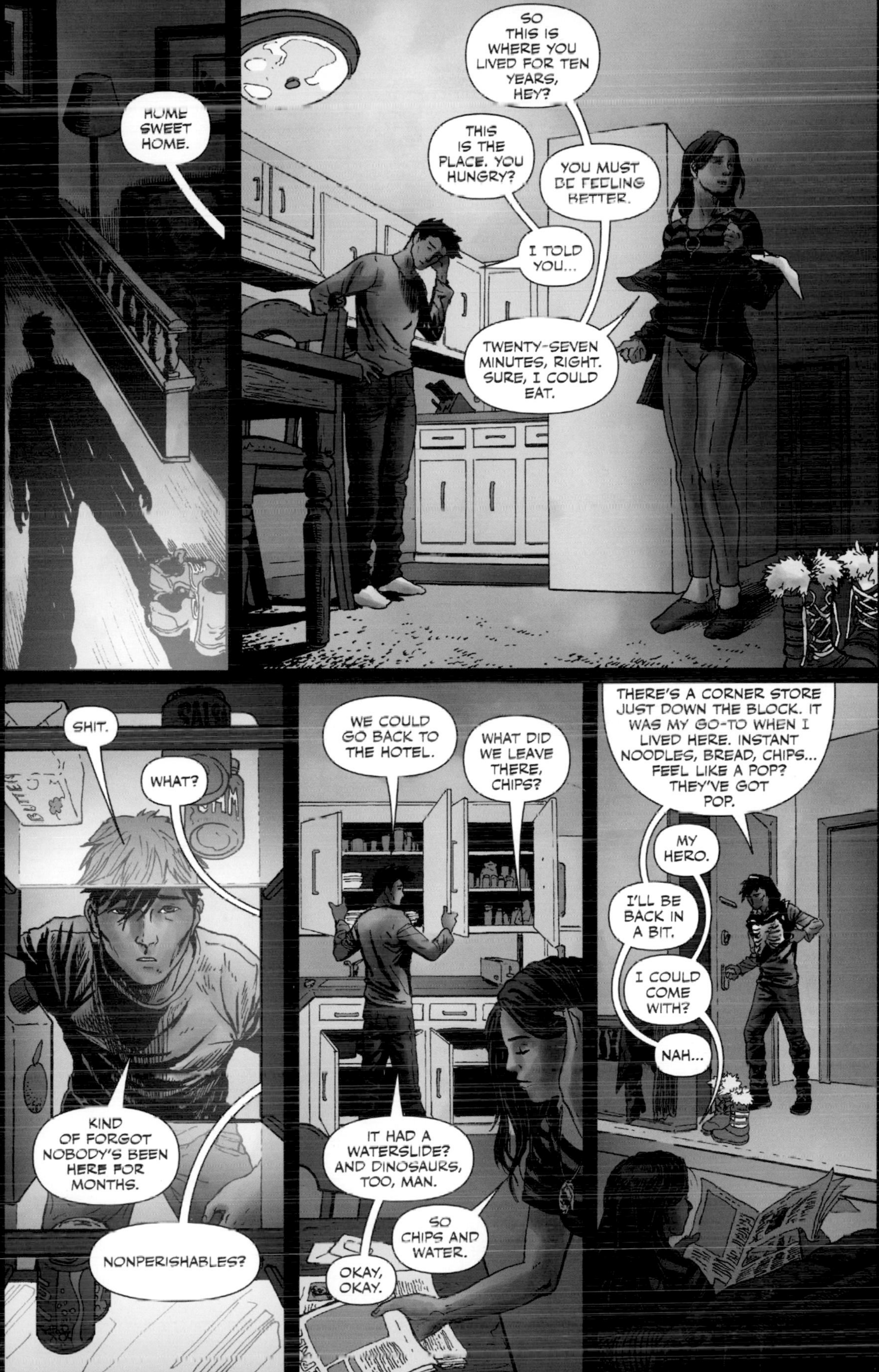
HOME SWEET HOME.
SO THIS IS WHERE YOU LIVED FOR TEN YEARS, HEY?
THIS IS THE PLACE. YOU HUNGRY?
YOU MUST BE FEELING BETTER.
I TOLD YOU...
TWENTY-SEVEN MINUTES, RIGHT. SURE, I COULD EAT.
SHIT.
WHAT?
KIND OF FORGOT NOBODY'S BEEN HERE FOR MONTHS.
NONPERISHABLES?
WE COULD GO BACK TO THE HOTEL.
WHAT DID WE LEAVE THERE, CHIPS?
IT HAD A WATERSLIDE? AND DINOSAURS, TOO, MAN.
SO CHIPS AND WATER.
OKAY, OKAY.
THERE'S A CORNER STORE JUST DOWN THE BLOCK. IT WAS MY GO-TO WHEN I LIVED HERE. INSTANT NOODLES, BREAD, CHIPS... FEEL LIKE A POP? THEY'VE GOT POP.
MY HERO.
I'LL BE BACK IN A BIT.
I COULD COME WITH?
NAH...

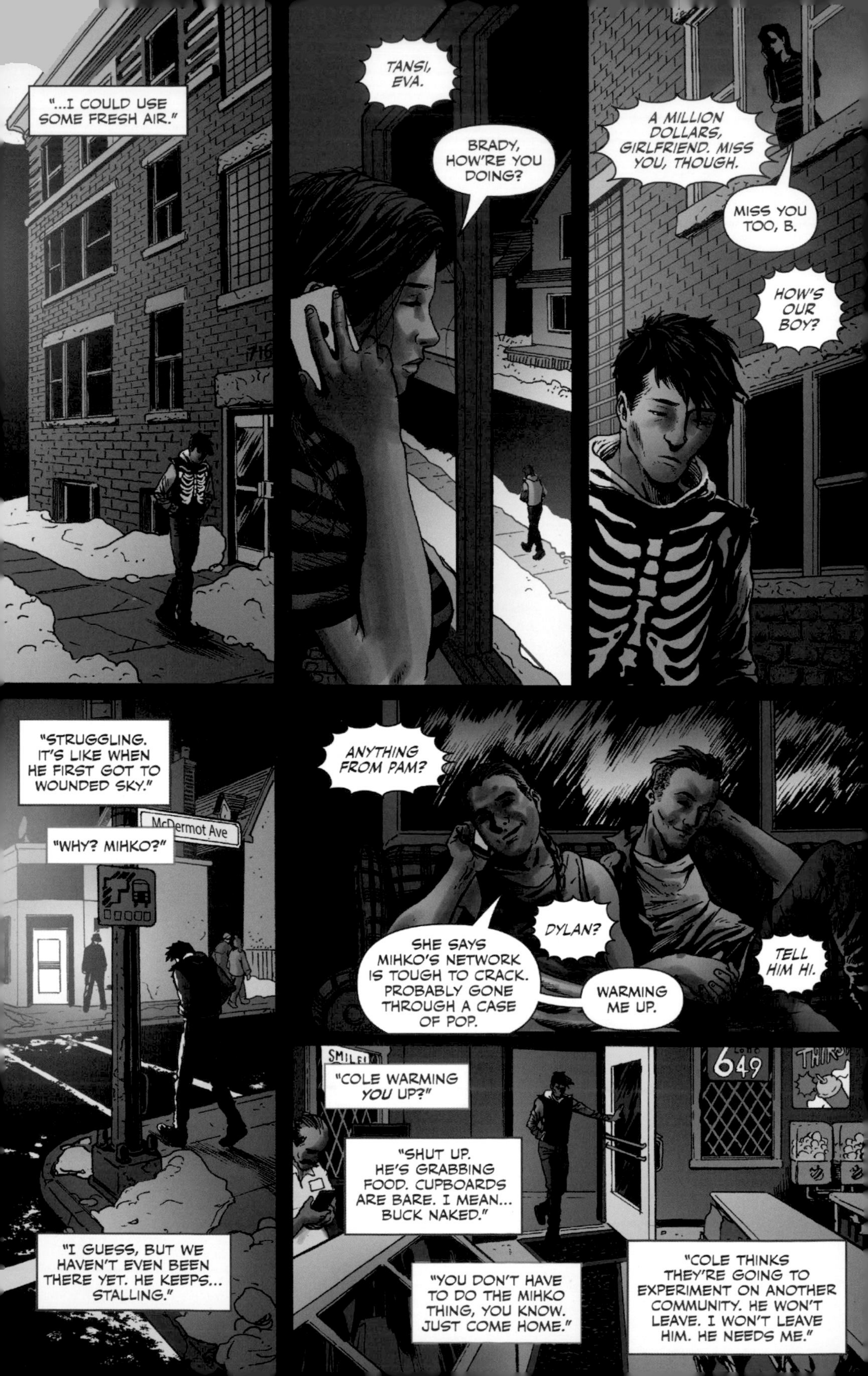
"...I COULD USE SOME FRESH AIR."
TANSI, EVA.
BRADY, HOW'RE YOU DOING?
A MILLION DOLLARS, GIRLFRIEND. MISS YOU, THOUGH.
MISS YOU TOO, B.
HOW'S OUR BOY?
"STRUGGLING. IT'S LIKE WHEN HE FIRST GOT TO WOUNDED SKY."
McDermot Ave
"WHY? MIHKO?"
"I GUESS, BUT WE HAVEN'T EVEN BEEN THERE YET. HE KEEPS... STALLING."
ANYTHING FROM PAM?
SHE SAYS MIHKO'S NETWORK IS TOUGH TO CRACK. PROBABLY GONE THROUGH A CASE OF POP.
DYLAN?
WARMING ME UP.
TELL HIM HI.
"COLE WARMING *YOU* UP?"
649
"SHUT UP. HE'S GRABBING FOOD. CUPBOARDS ARE BARE. I MEAN... BUCK NAKED."
"YOU DON'T HAVE TO DO THE MIHKO THING, YOU KNOW. JUST COME HOME."
"COLE THINKS THEY'RE GOING TO EXPERIMENT ON ANOTHER COMMUNITY. HE WON'T LEAVE. I WON'T LEAVE HIM. HE NEEDS ME."

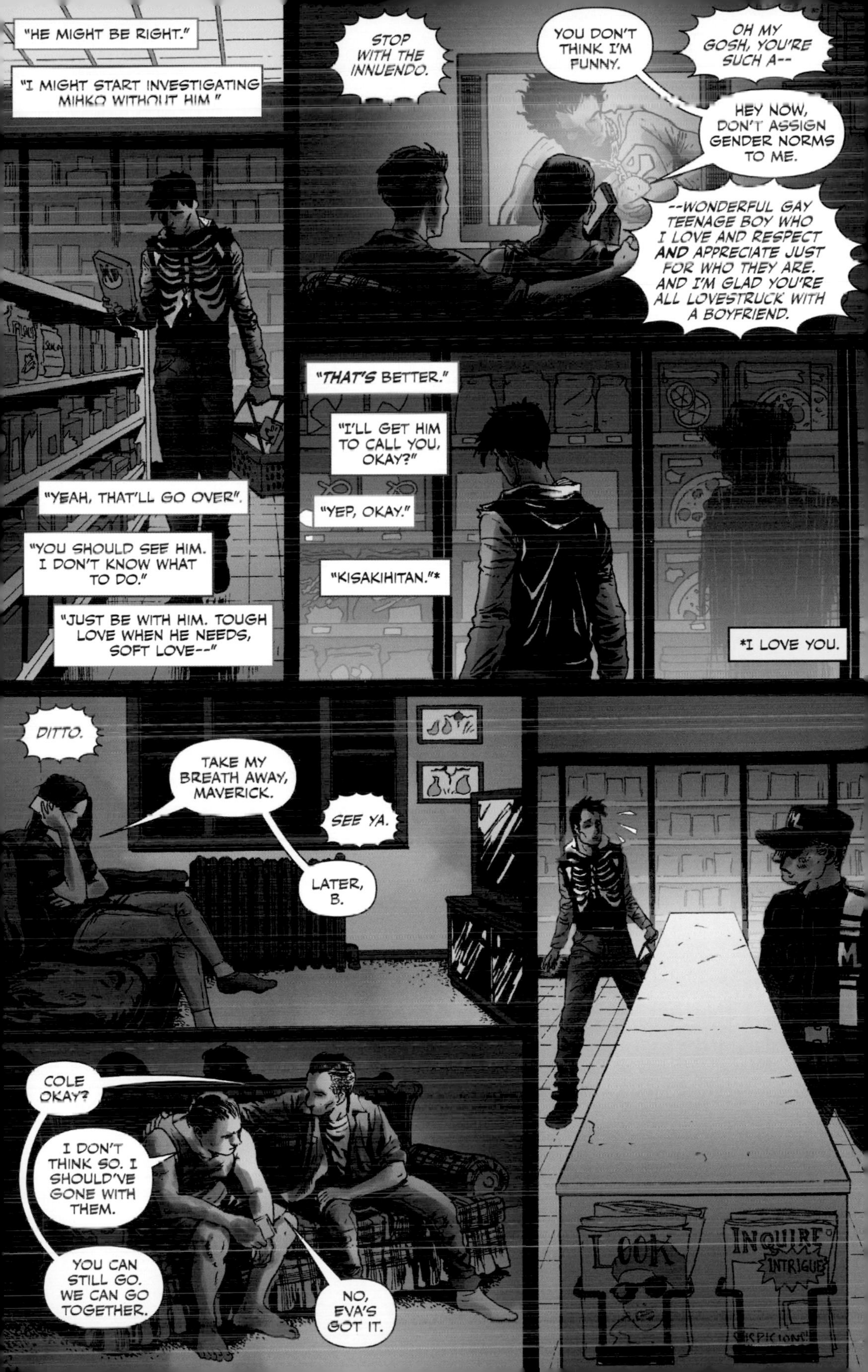
"HE MIGHT BE RIGHT."
"I MIGHT START INVESTIGATING MIHKO WITHOUT HIM."
STOP WITH THE INNUENDO.
YOU DON'T THINK I'M FUNNY.
OH MY GOSH, YOU'RE SUCH A--
HEY NOW, DON'T ASSIGN GENDER NORMS TO ME.
--WONDERFUL GAY TEENAGE BOY WHO I LOVE AND RESPECT AND APPRECIATE JUST FOR WHO THEY ARE. AND I'M GLAD YOU'RE ALL LOVESTRUCK WITH A BOYFRIEND.
"YEAH, THAT'LL GO OVER".
"YOU SHOULD SEE HIM. I DON'T KNOW WHAT TO DO."
"JUST BE WITH HIM. TOUGH LOVE WHEN HE NEEDS, SOFT LOVE--"
"THAT'S BETTER."
"I'LL GET HIM TO CALL YOU, OKAY?"
"YEP, OKAY."
"KISAKIHITAN."*
*I LOVE YOU.
DITTO.
TAKE MY BREATH AWAY, MAVERICK.
SEE YA.
LATER, B.
COLE OKAY?
I DON'T THINK SO. I SHOULD'VE GONE WITH THEM.
YOU CAN STILL GO. WE CAN GO TOGETHER.
NO, EVA'S GOT IT.
LOOK
INQUIRE
INTRIGUE

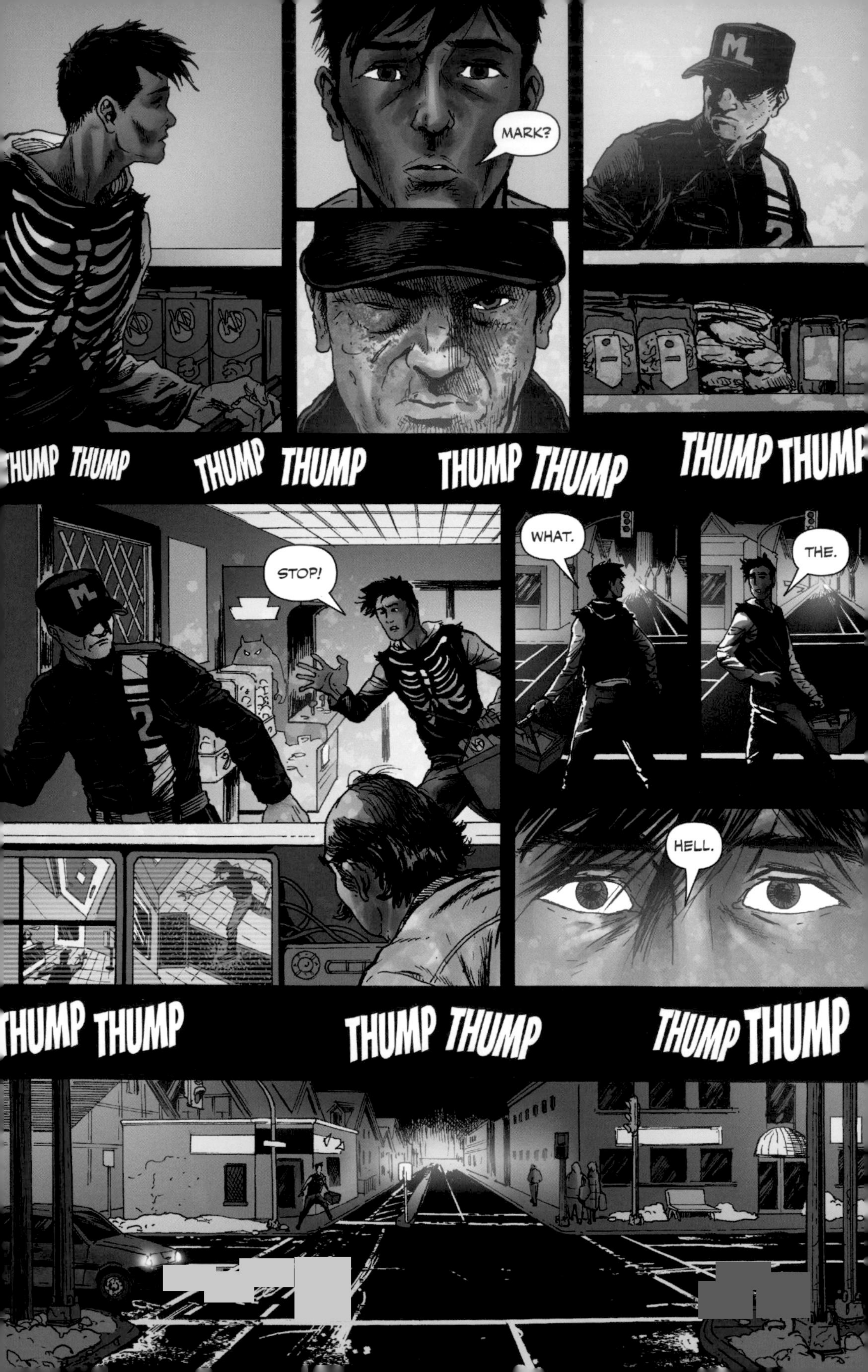
MARK?
THUMP THUMP
THUMP THUMP
THUMP THUMP
THUMP THUMP
STOP!
WHAT.
THE.
HELL.
THUMP THUMP
THUMP THUMP
THUMP THUMP

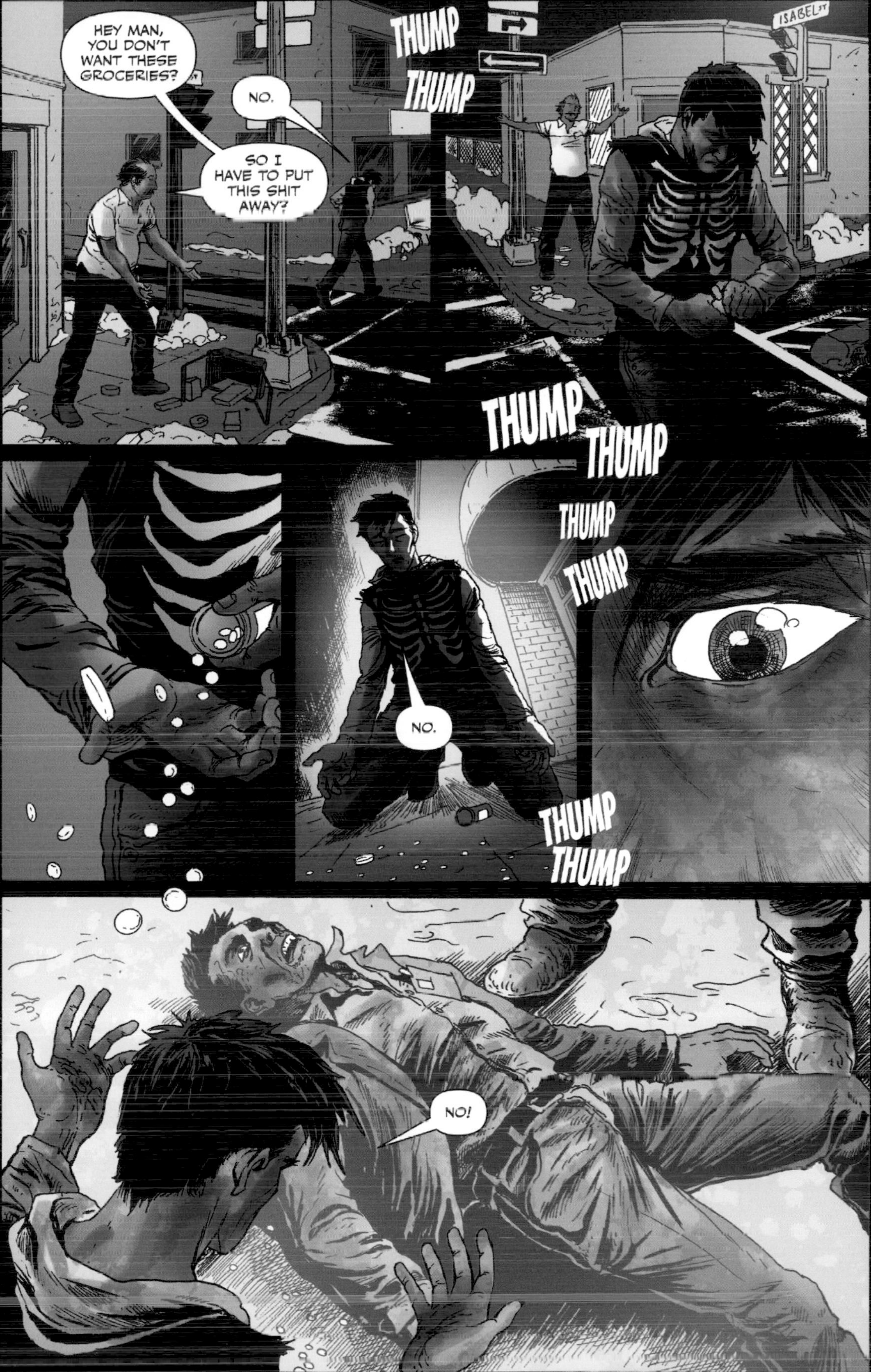
HEY MAN, YOU DON'T WANT THESE GROCERIES?
NO.
SO I HAVE TO PUT THIS SHIT AWAY?
ISABEL ST
THUMP
THUMP
THUMP
THUMP
THUMP
THUMP
NO.
THUMP
THUMP
NO!

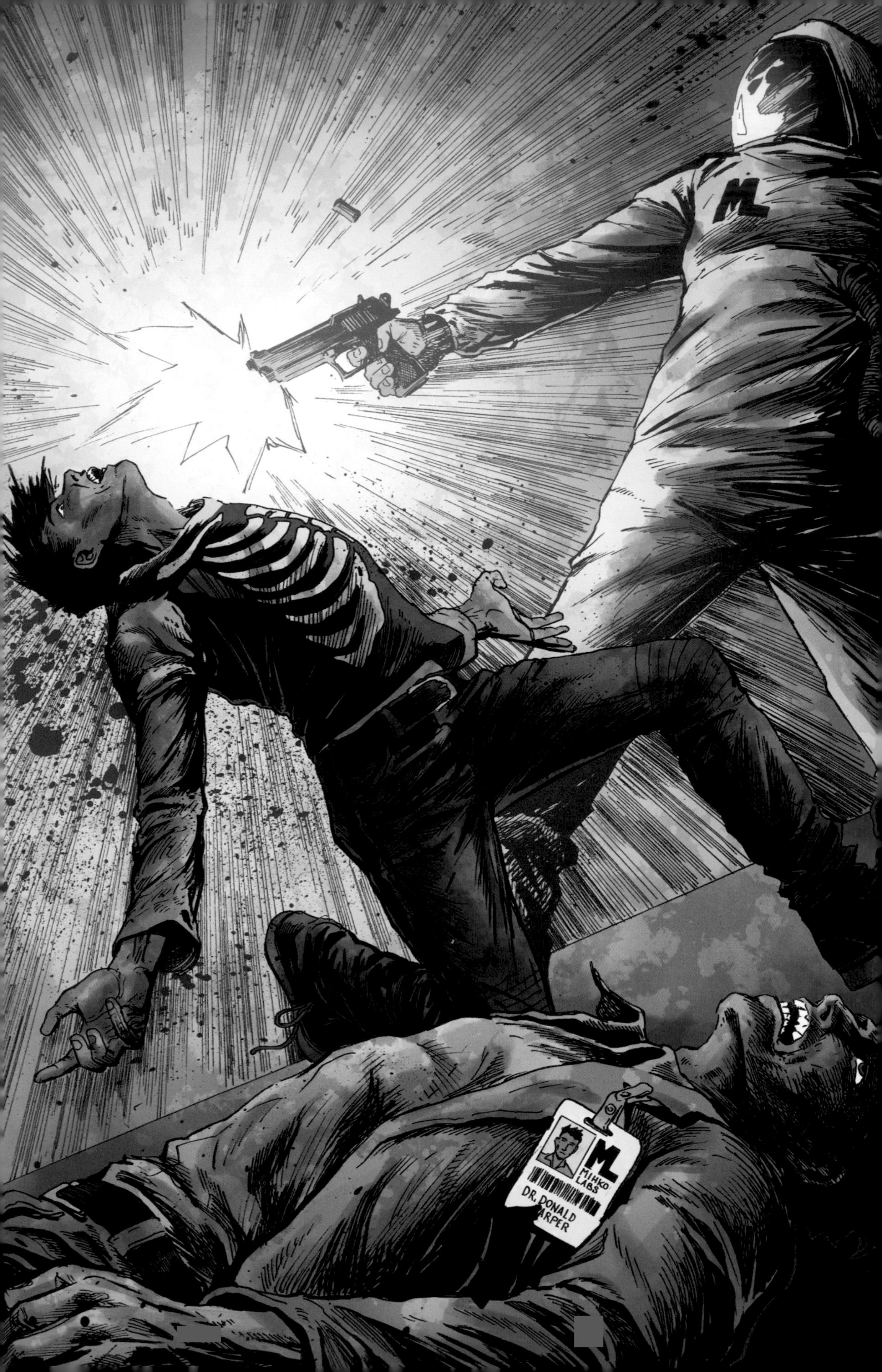
MIHKO LABS
DR. DONALD
ARPER

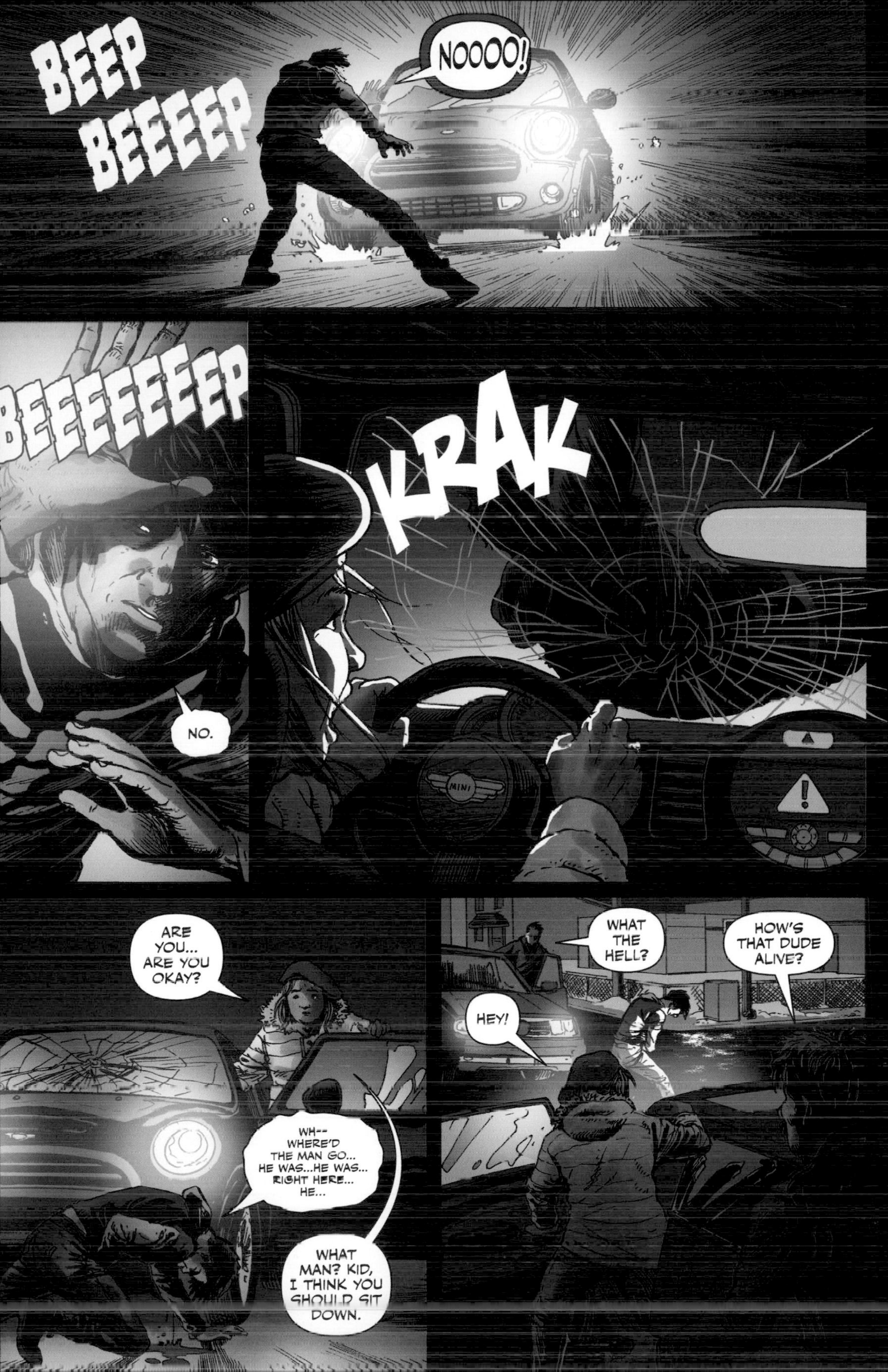
BEEP
BEEEEEP
NOOOO!
BEEEEEEEP
NO.
KRAK
ARE YOU... ARE YOU OKAY?
WH-- WHERE'D THE MAN GO... HE WAS...HE WAS... RIGHT HERE... HE...
WHAT MAN? KID, I THINK YOU SHOULD SIT DOWN.
WHAT THE HELL?
HOW'S THAT DUDE ALIVE?
HEY!

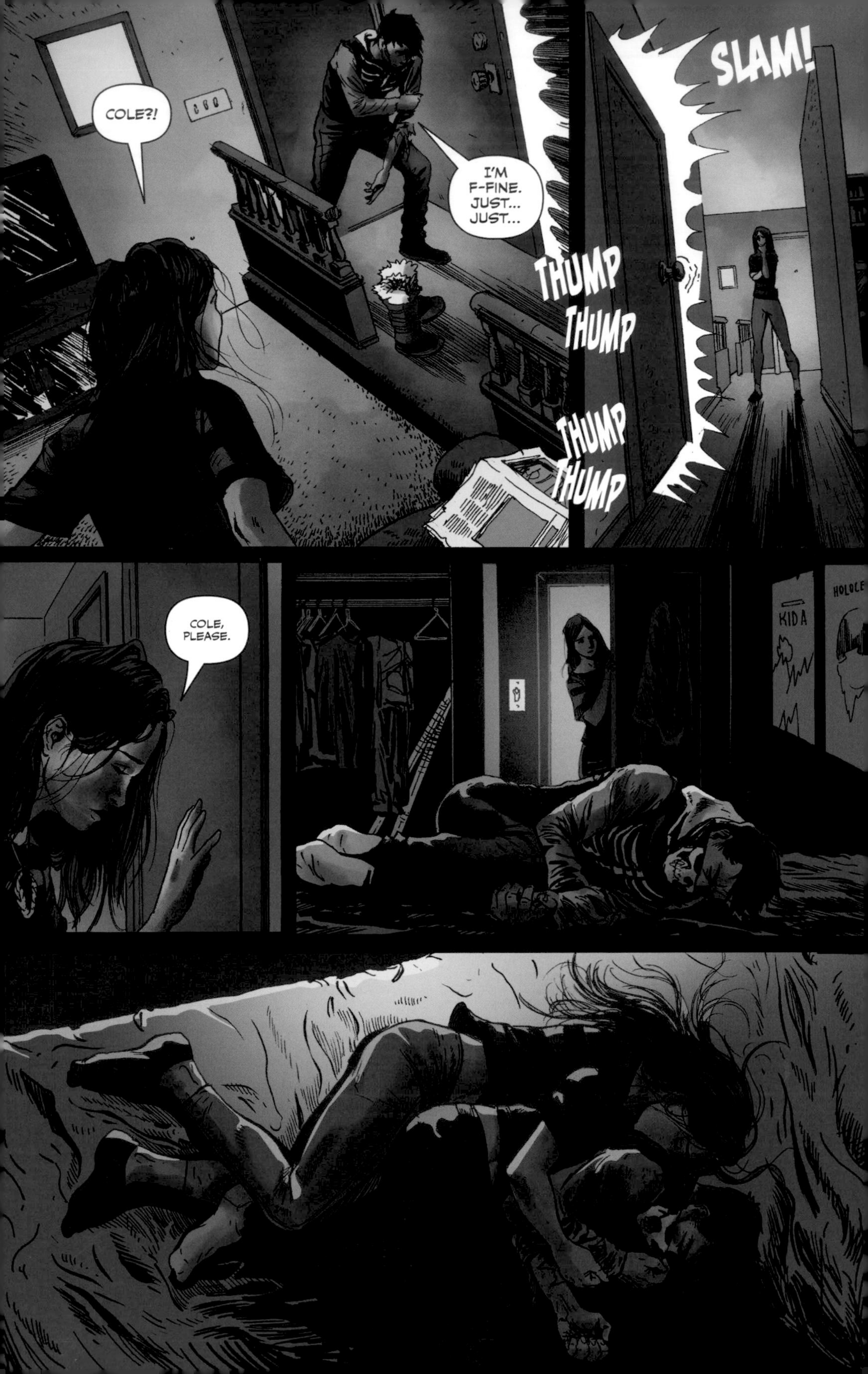
COLE?!
I'M F-FINE. JUST... JUST...
THUMP
THUMP
THUMP
THUMP
SLAM!
COLE, PLEASE.
KID A

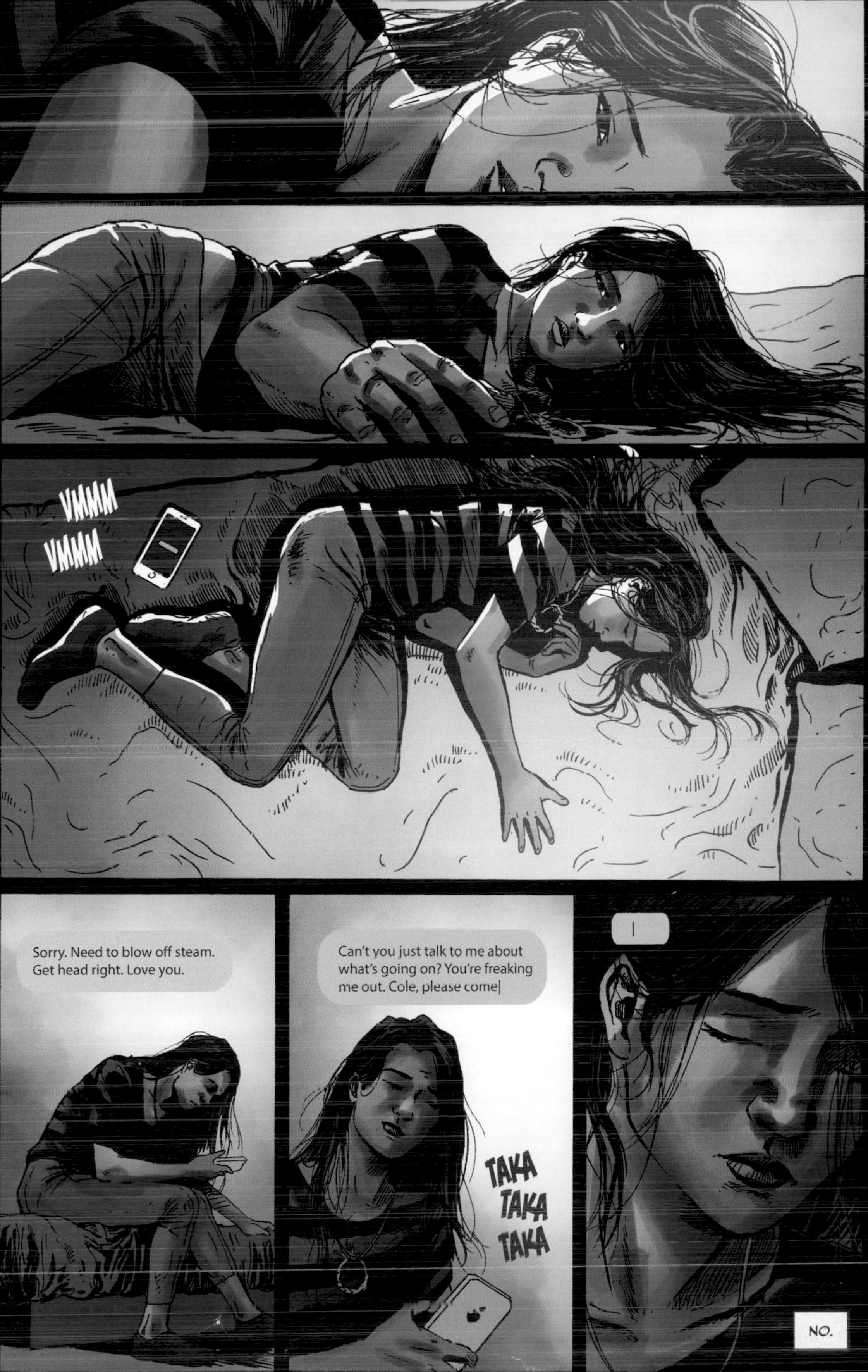
VMMM
VMMM
Sorry. Need to blow off steam. Get head right. Love you.
Can't you just talk to me about what's going on? You're freaking me out. Cole, please come|
TAKA
TAKA
TAKA
I
NO.

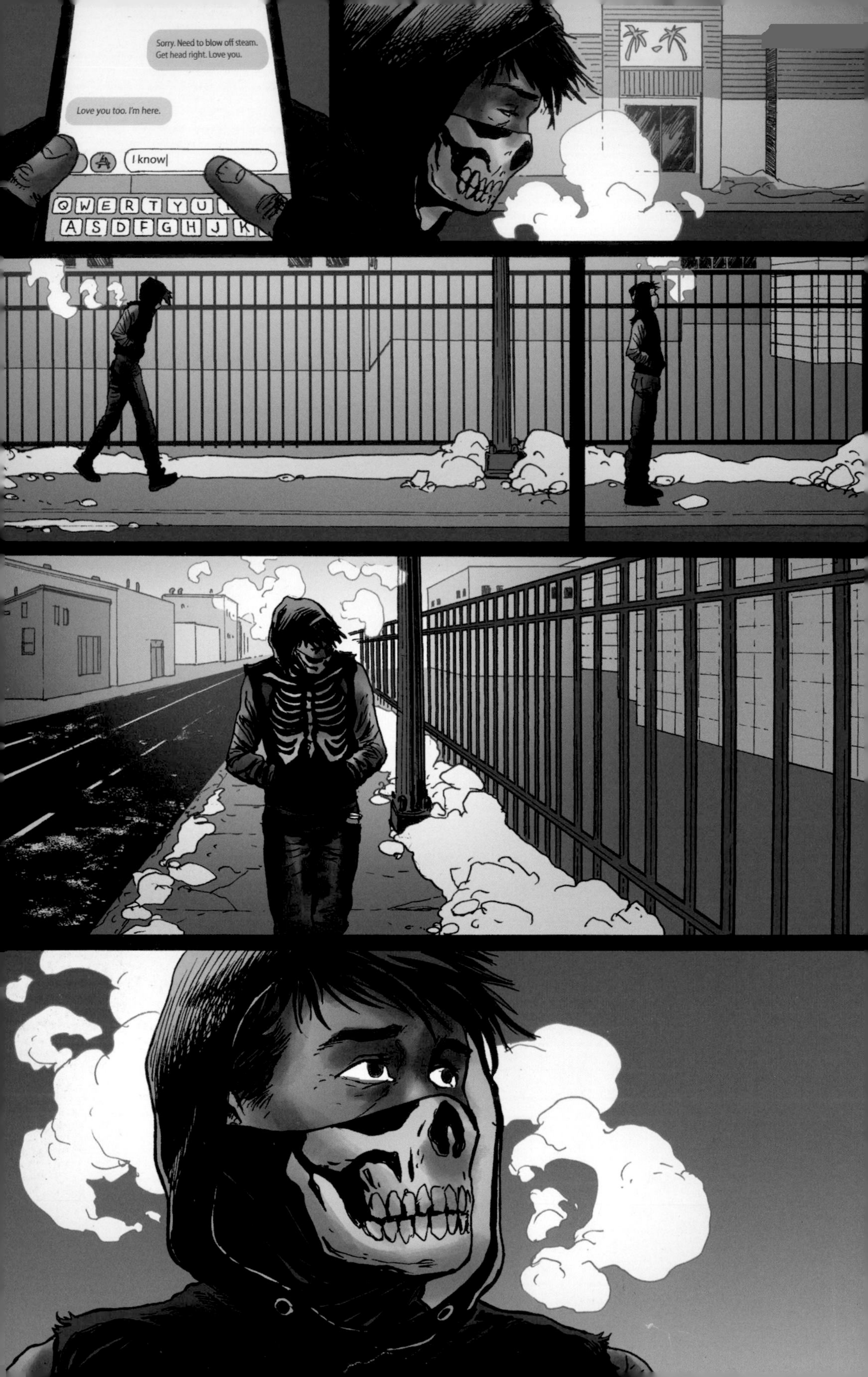
Sorry. Need to blow off steam. Get head right. Love you.
Love you too. I'm here.
I know

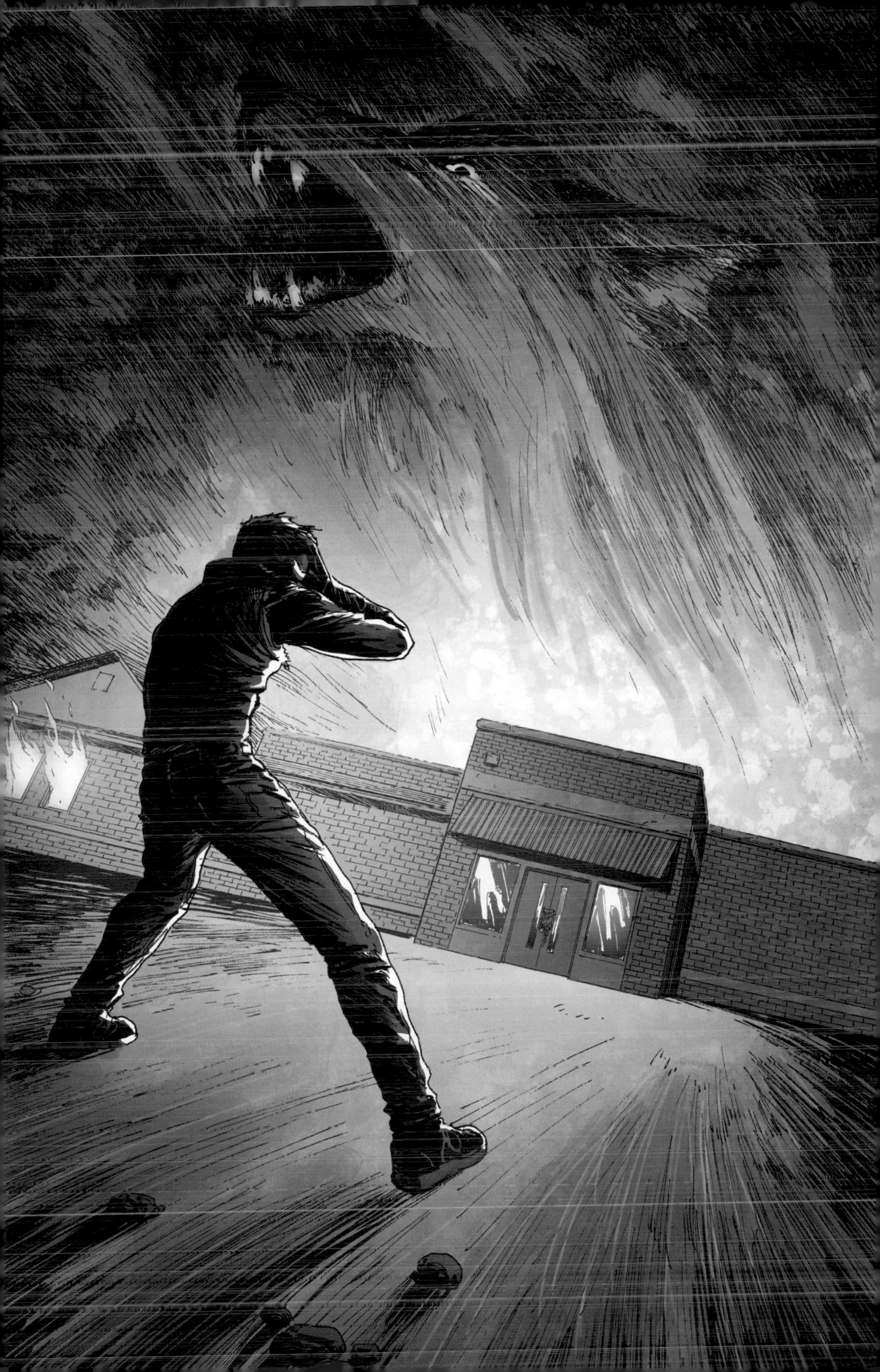

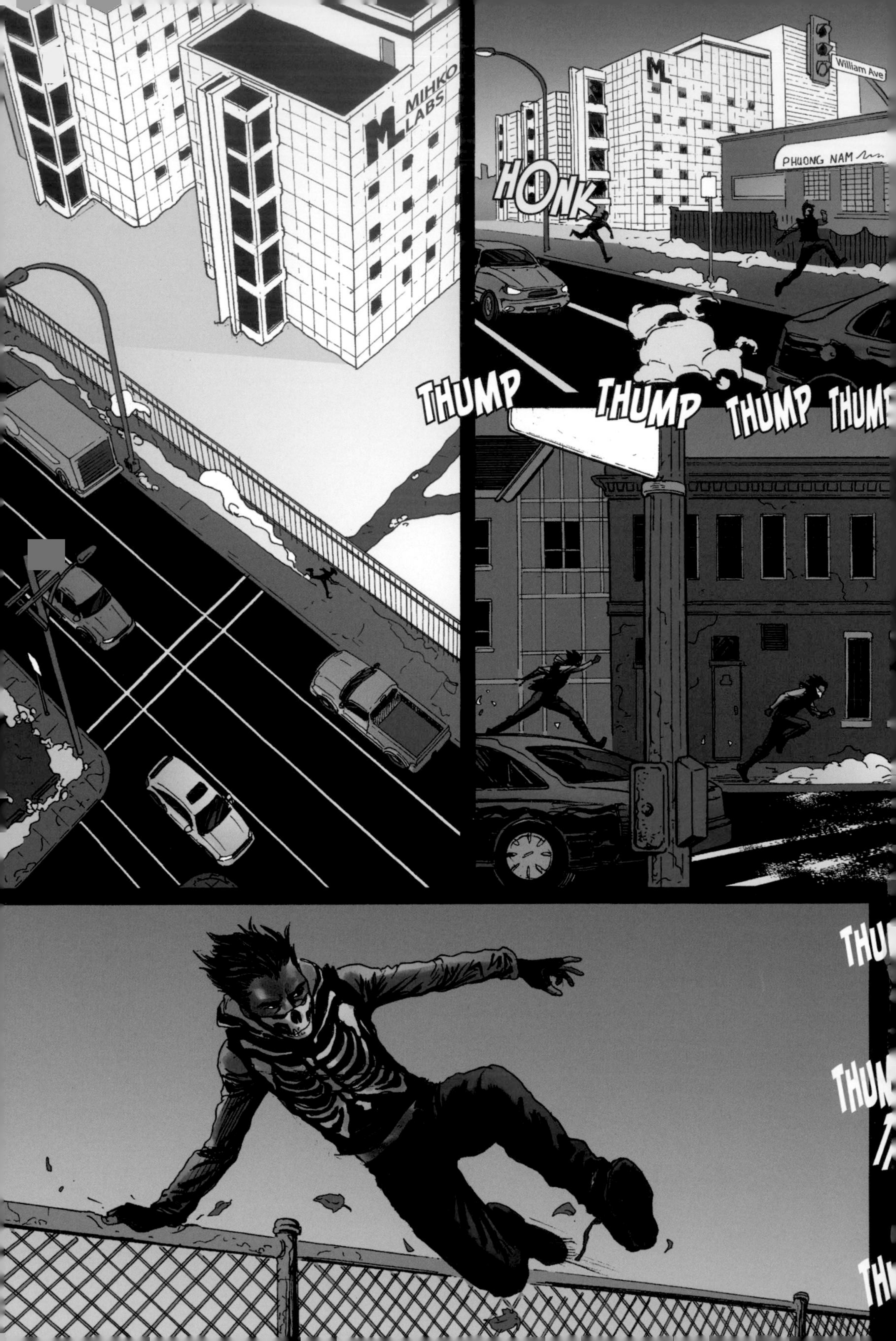

MIHKO LABS
ML
ML
William Ave
PHUONG NAM
HONK
THUMP
THUMP
THUMP
THUM
THU
THU
TH

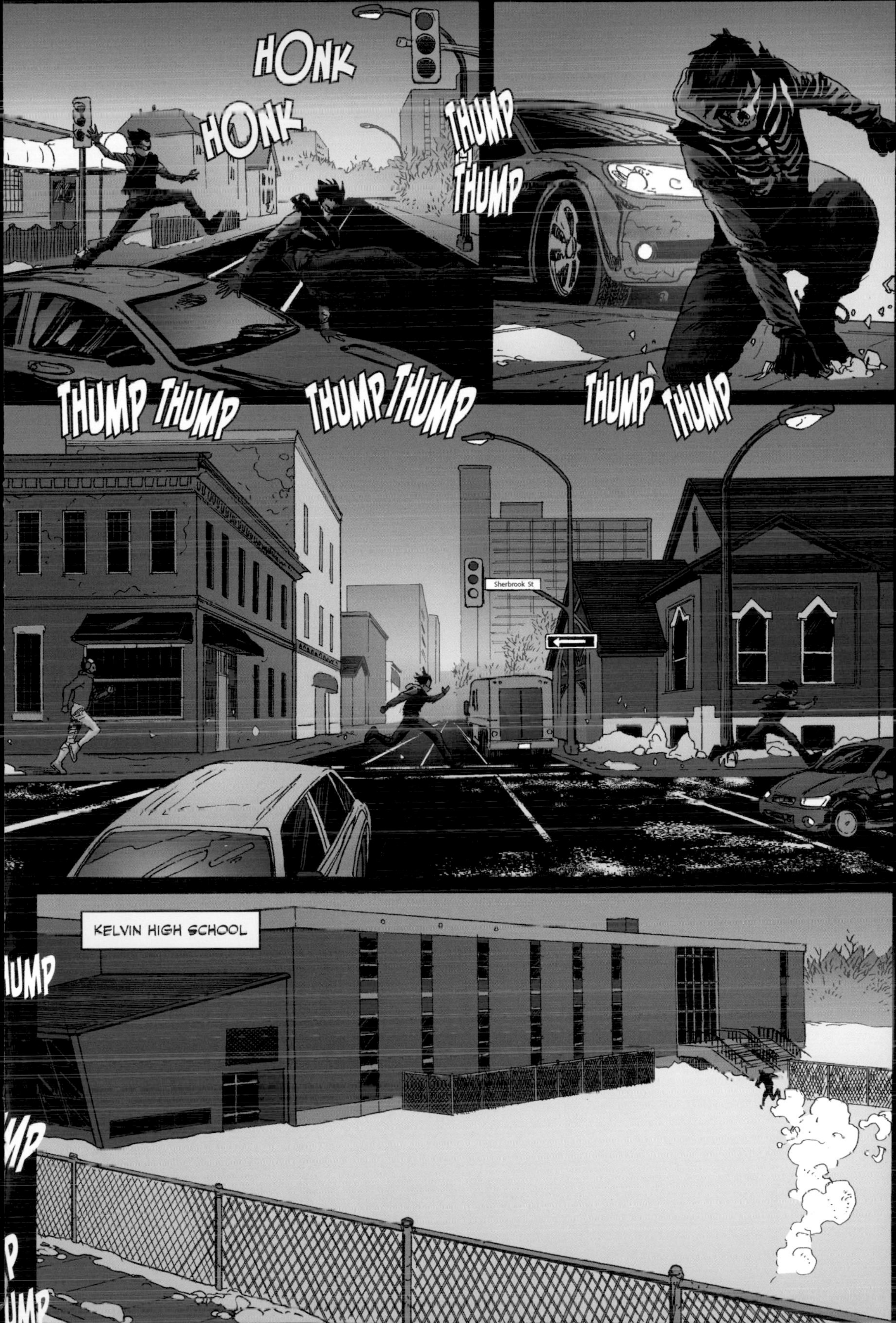

HONK
HONK
THUMP THUMP
THUMP THUMP
THUMP THUMP
THUMP THUMP
Sherbrook St
KELVIN HIGH SCHOOL

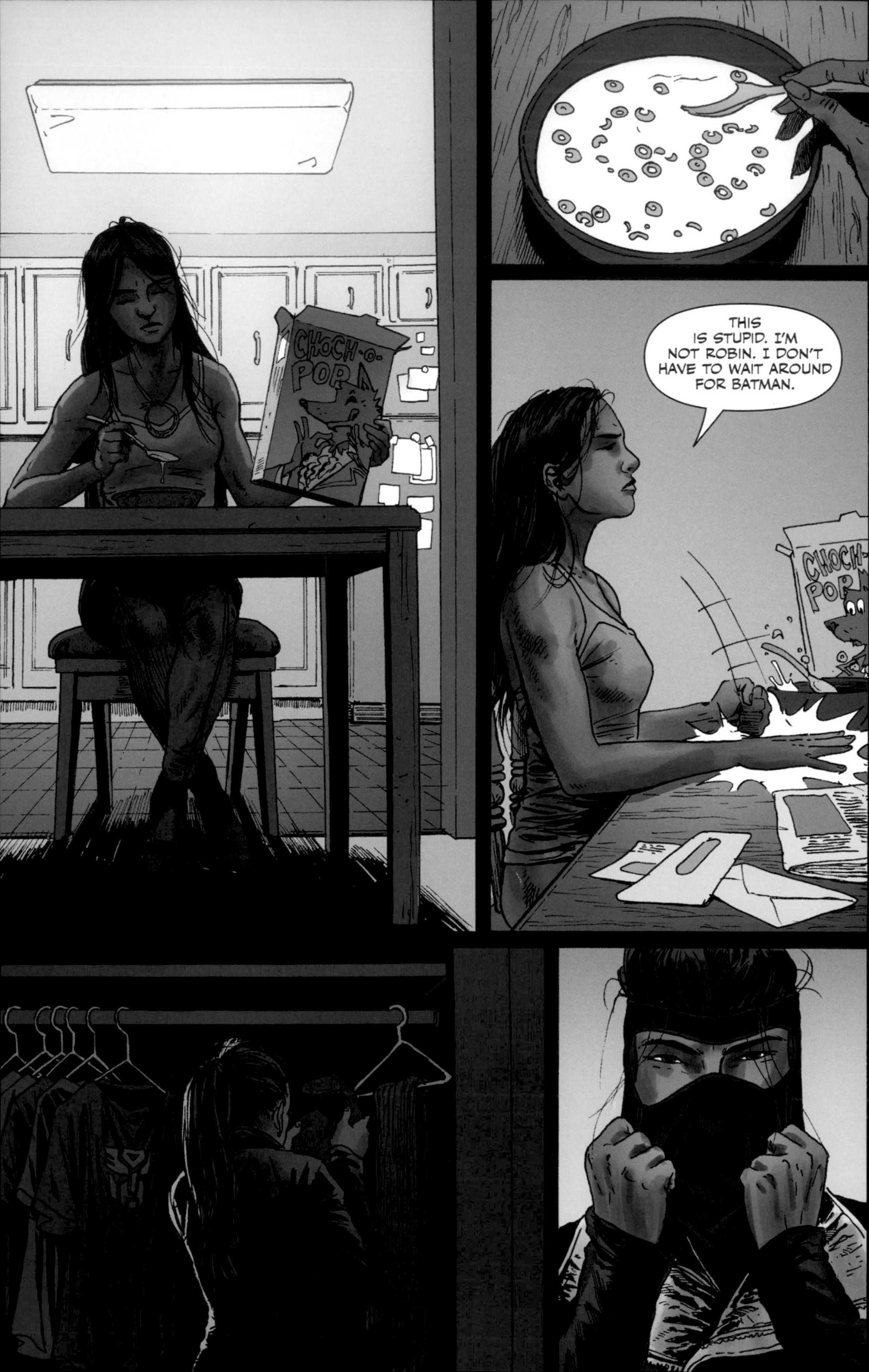
CHOCH-O-POP
THIS IS STUPID. I'M NOT ROBIN. I DON'T HAVE TO WAIT AROUND FOR BATMAN.
CHOCH-POP

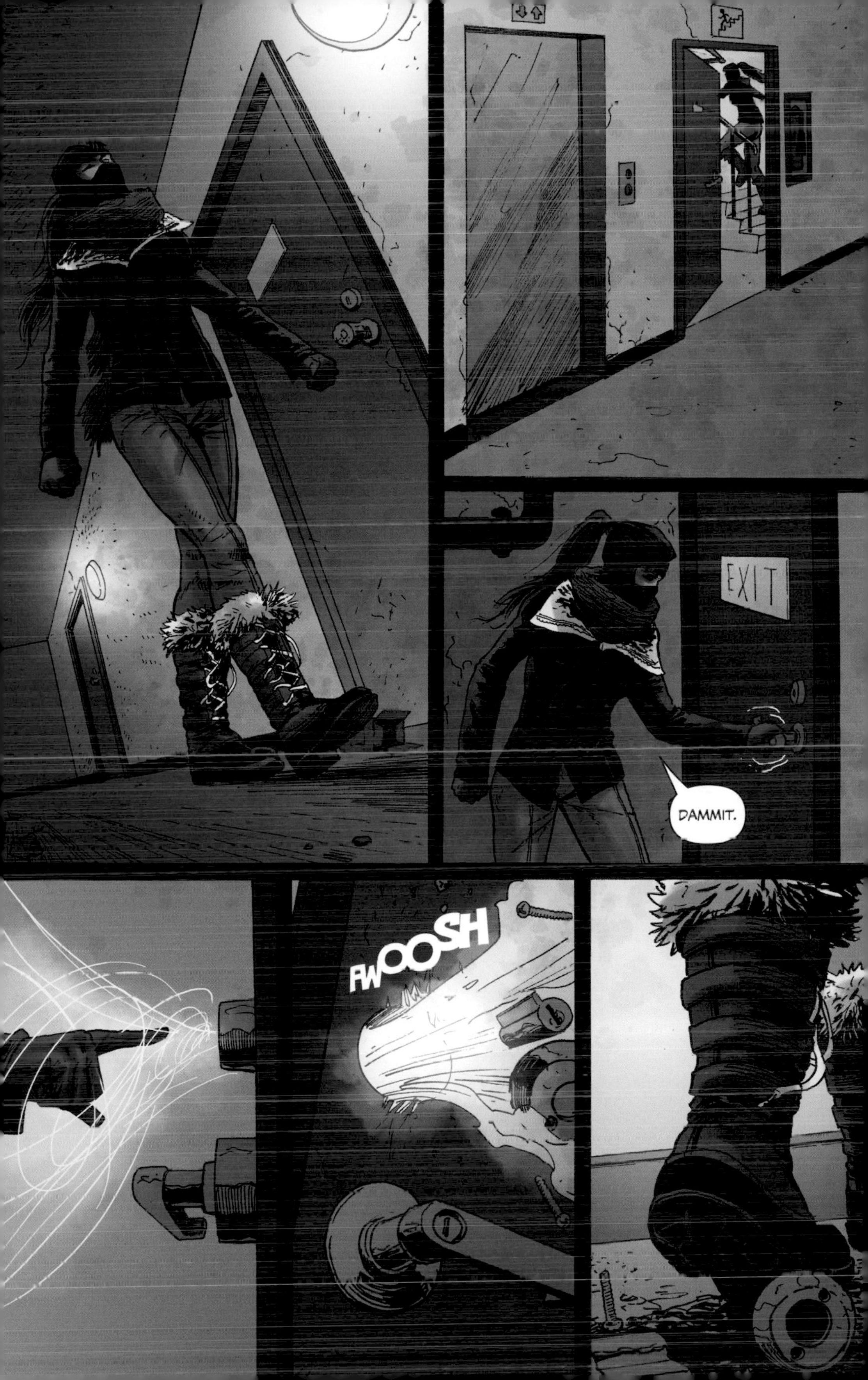
EXIT
DAMMIT.
FWOOSH

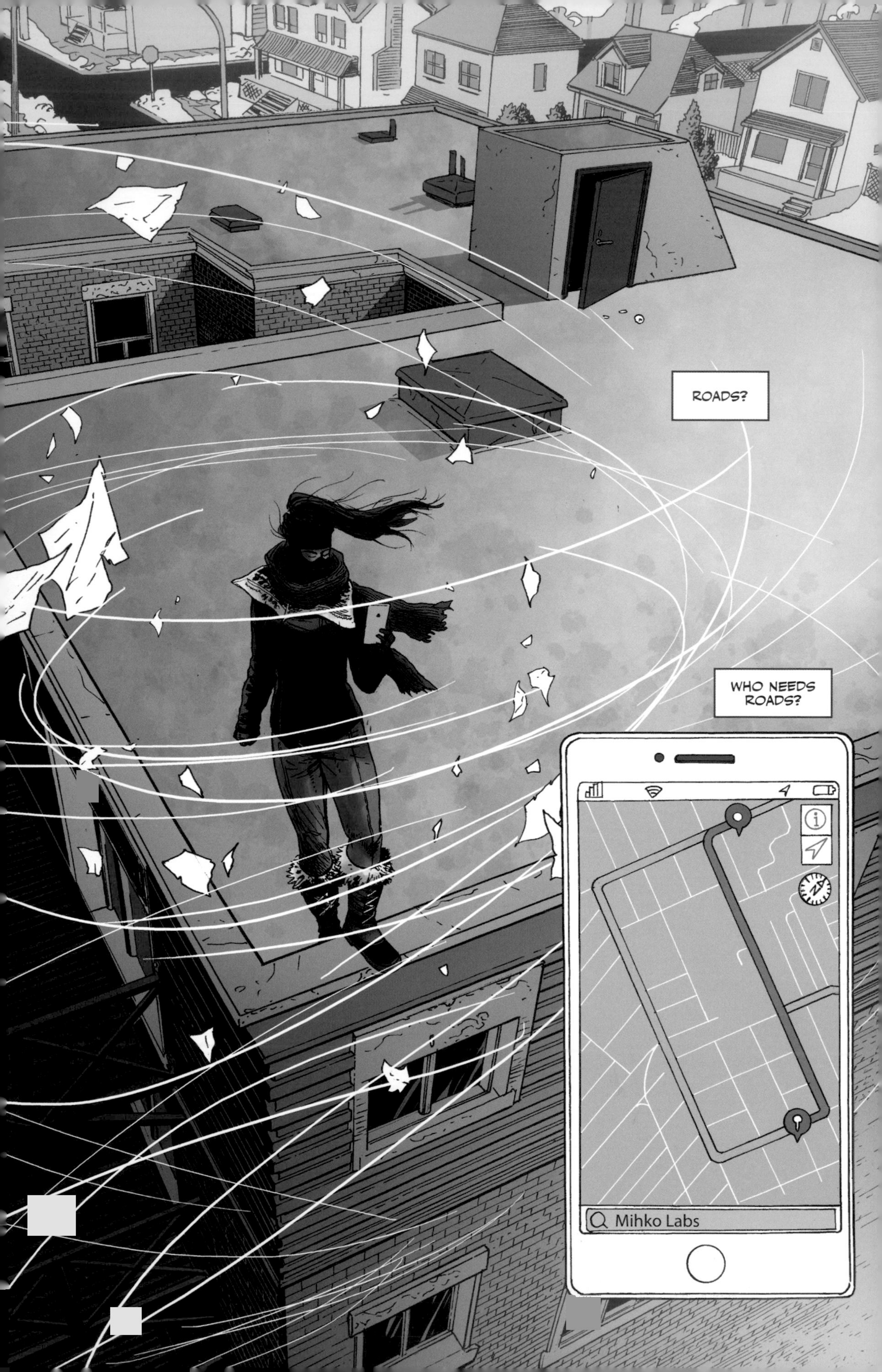
ROADS?
WHO NEEDS ROADS?
Mihko Labs

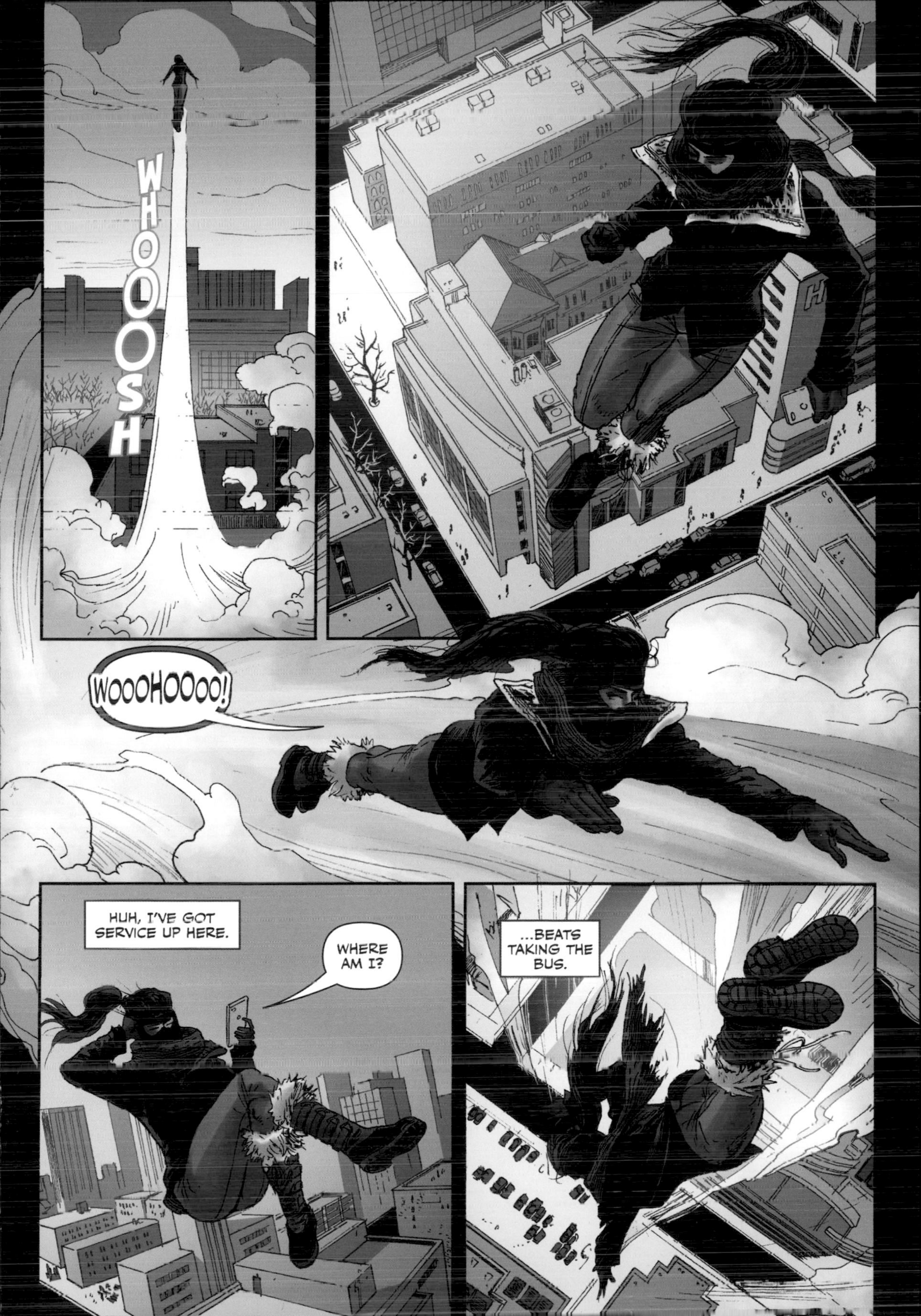
WHOOOOSH
WOOOHOOOO!
HUH, I'VE GOT SERVICE UP HERE.
WHERE AM I?
...BEATS TAKING THE BUS.

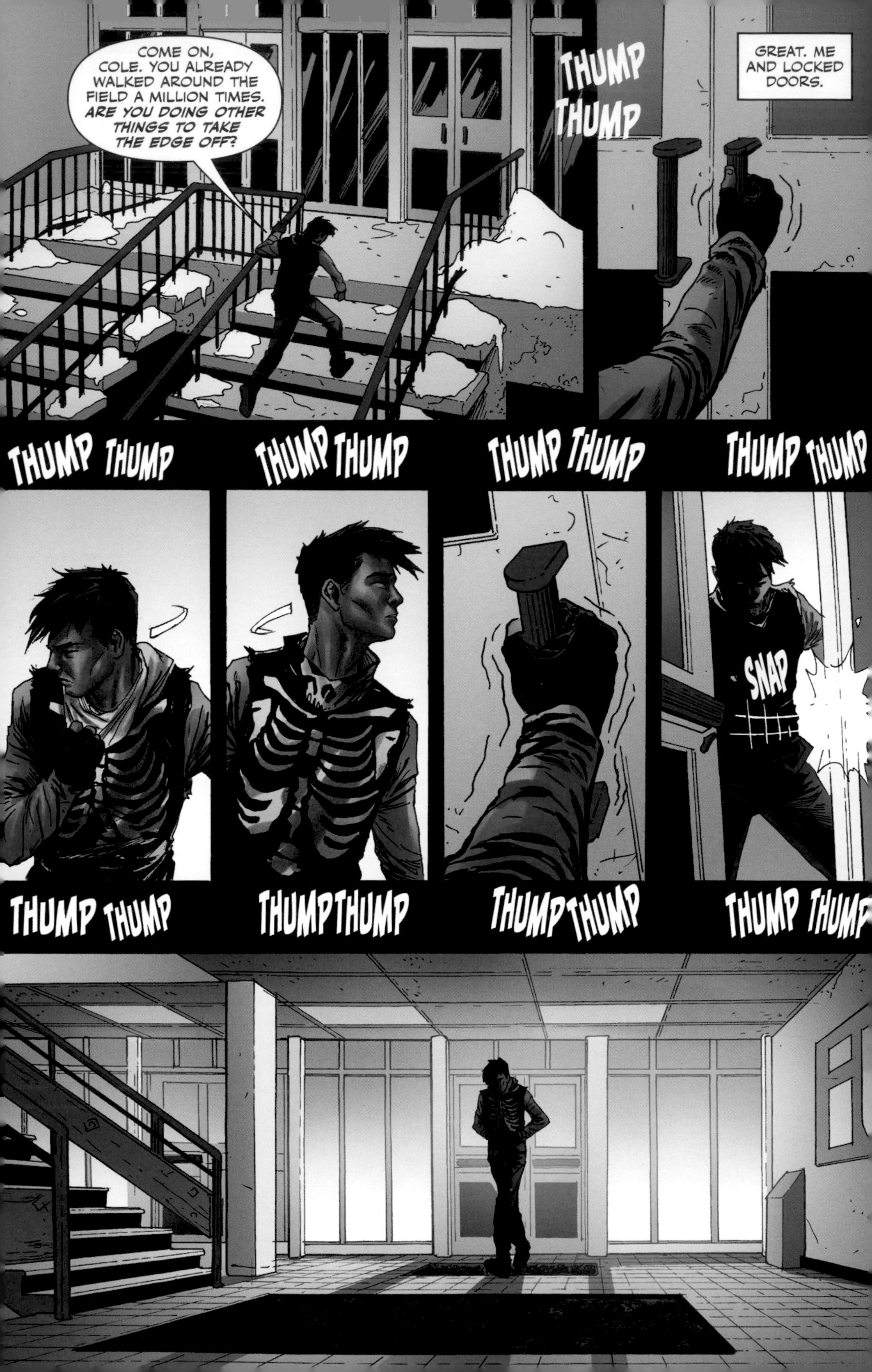

COME ON, COLE. YOU ALREADY WALKED AROUND THE FIELD A MILLION TIMES. ARE YOU DOING OTHER THINGS TO TAKE THE EDGE OFF?
THUMP THUMP
GREAT. ME AND LOCKED DOORS.
THUMP THUMP
THUMP THUMP
THUMP THUMP
THUMP THUMP
SNAP
THUMP THUMP
THUMP THUMP
THUMP THUMP
THUMP THUMP

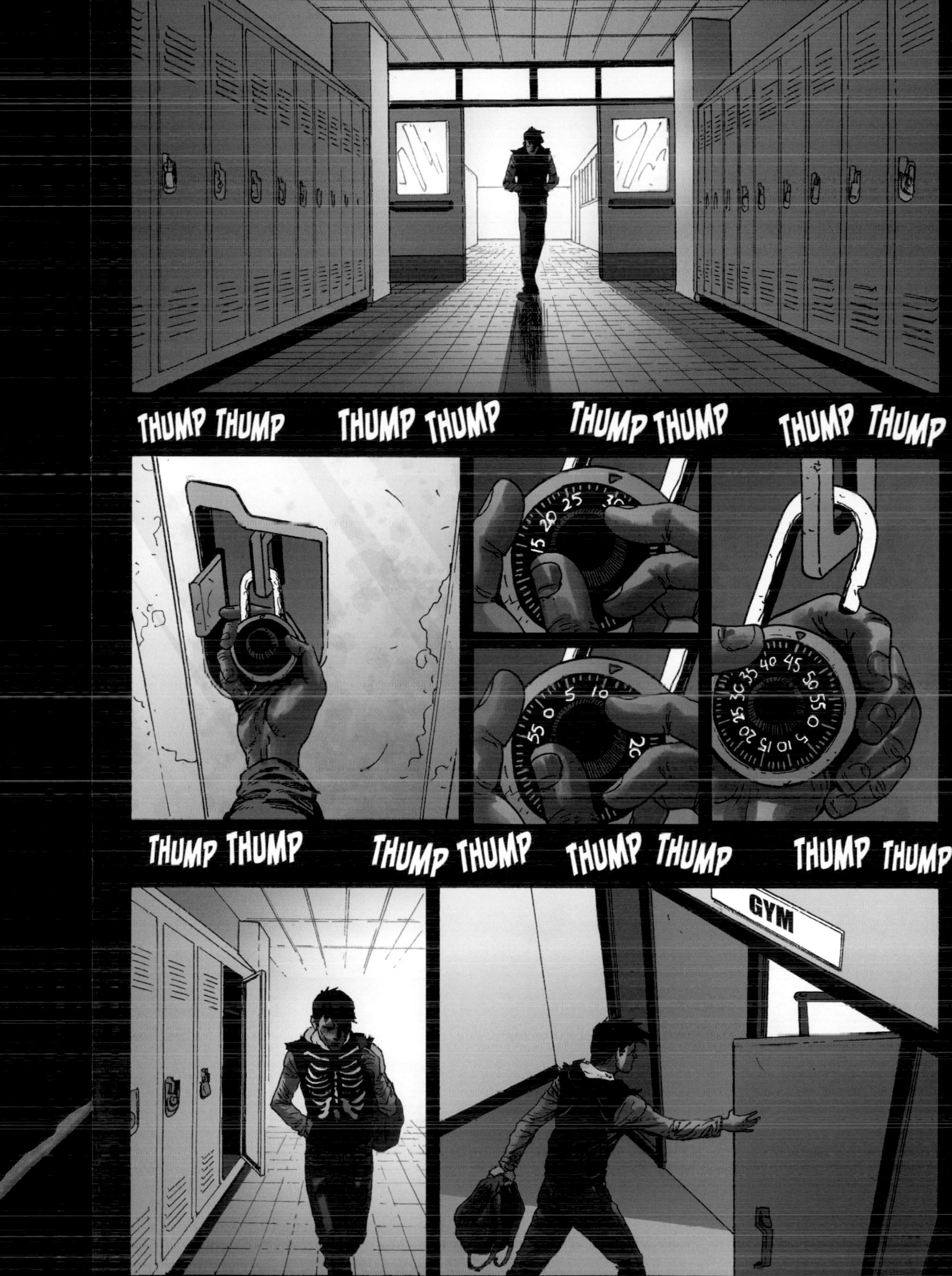
THUMP THUMP
THUMP THUMP
THUMP THUMP
THUMP THUMP
THUMP THUMP
THUMP THUMP
THUMP THUMP
THUMP THUMP
GYM

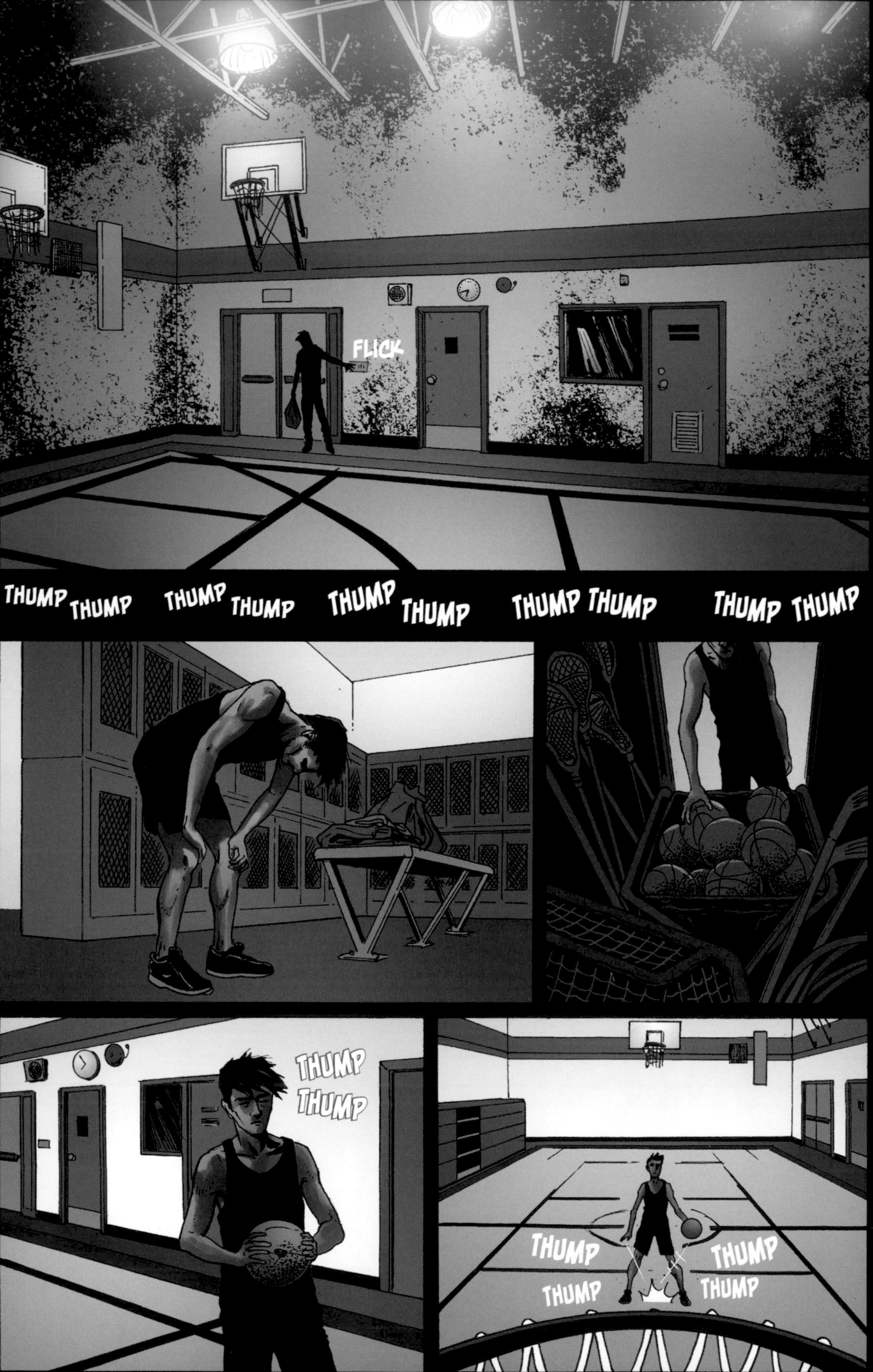
FLICK
THUMP THUMP THUMP THUMP THUMP THUMP THUMP THUMP THUMP THUMP
THUMP
THUMP
THUMP
THUMP
THUMP
THUMP

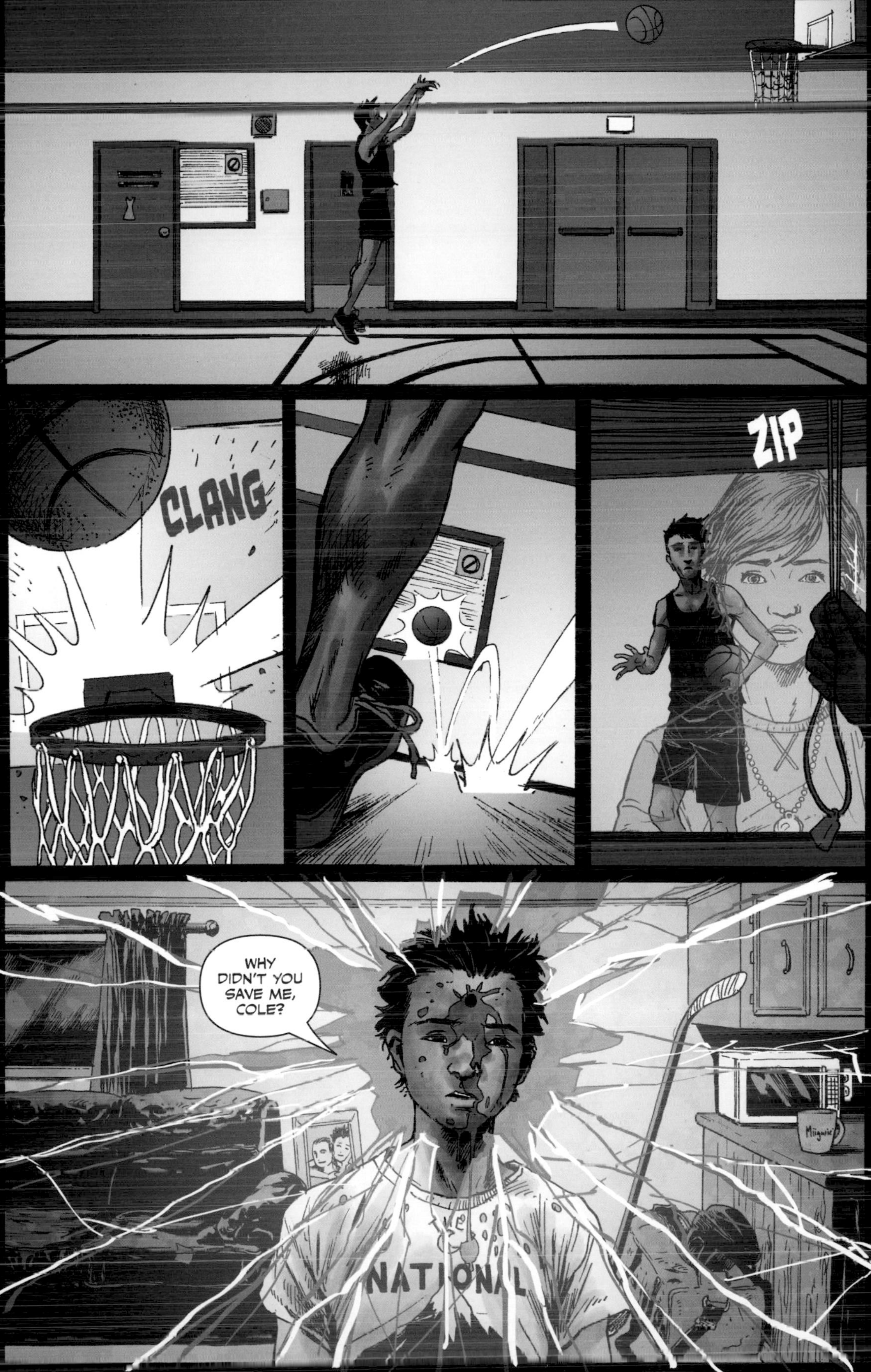
CLANG
ZIP
WHY DIDN'T YOU SAVE ME, COLE?
NATIONAL

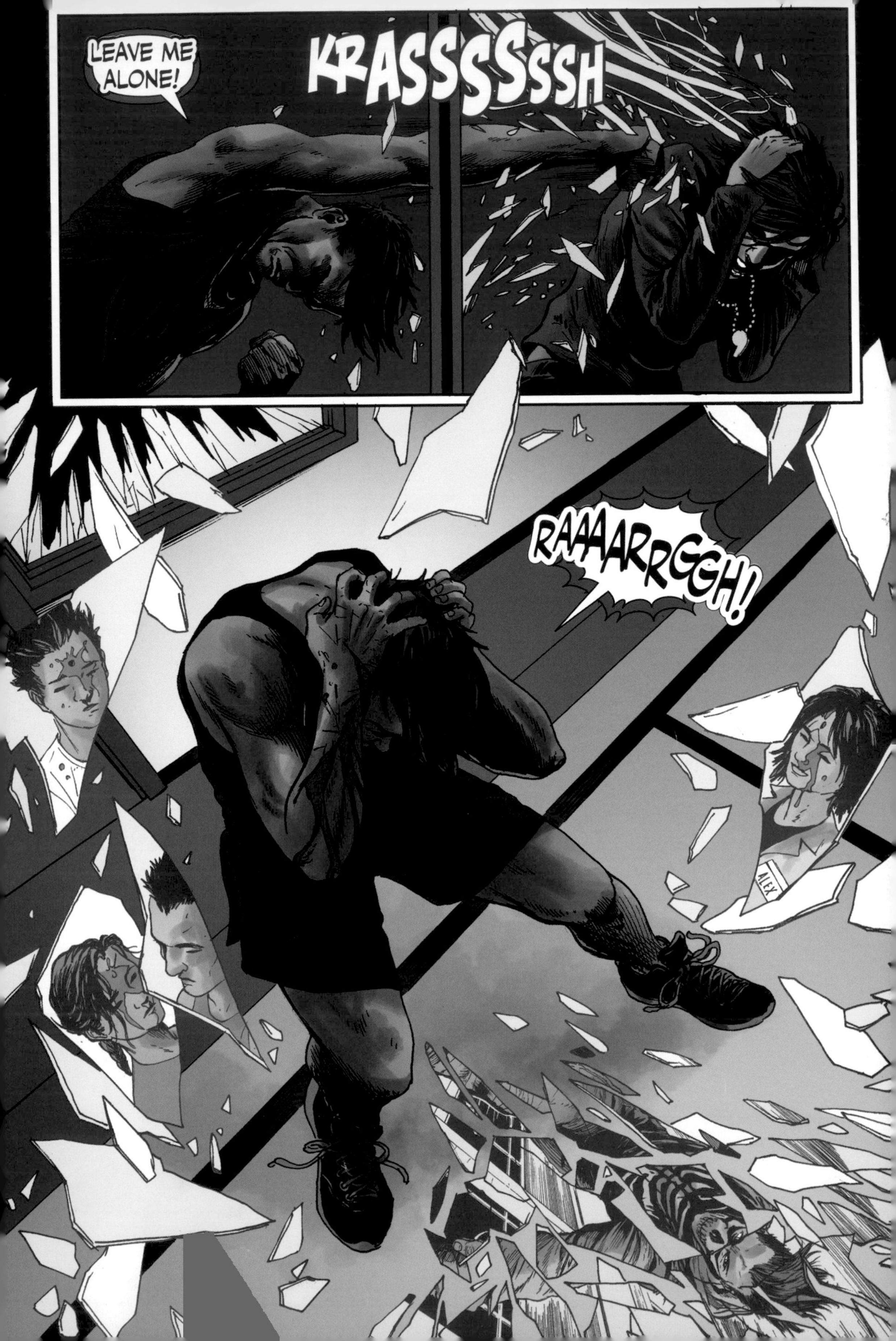
LEAVE ME ALONE!
KRASSSSSSSH
RAAAARRGGH!
ALEX

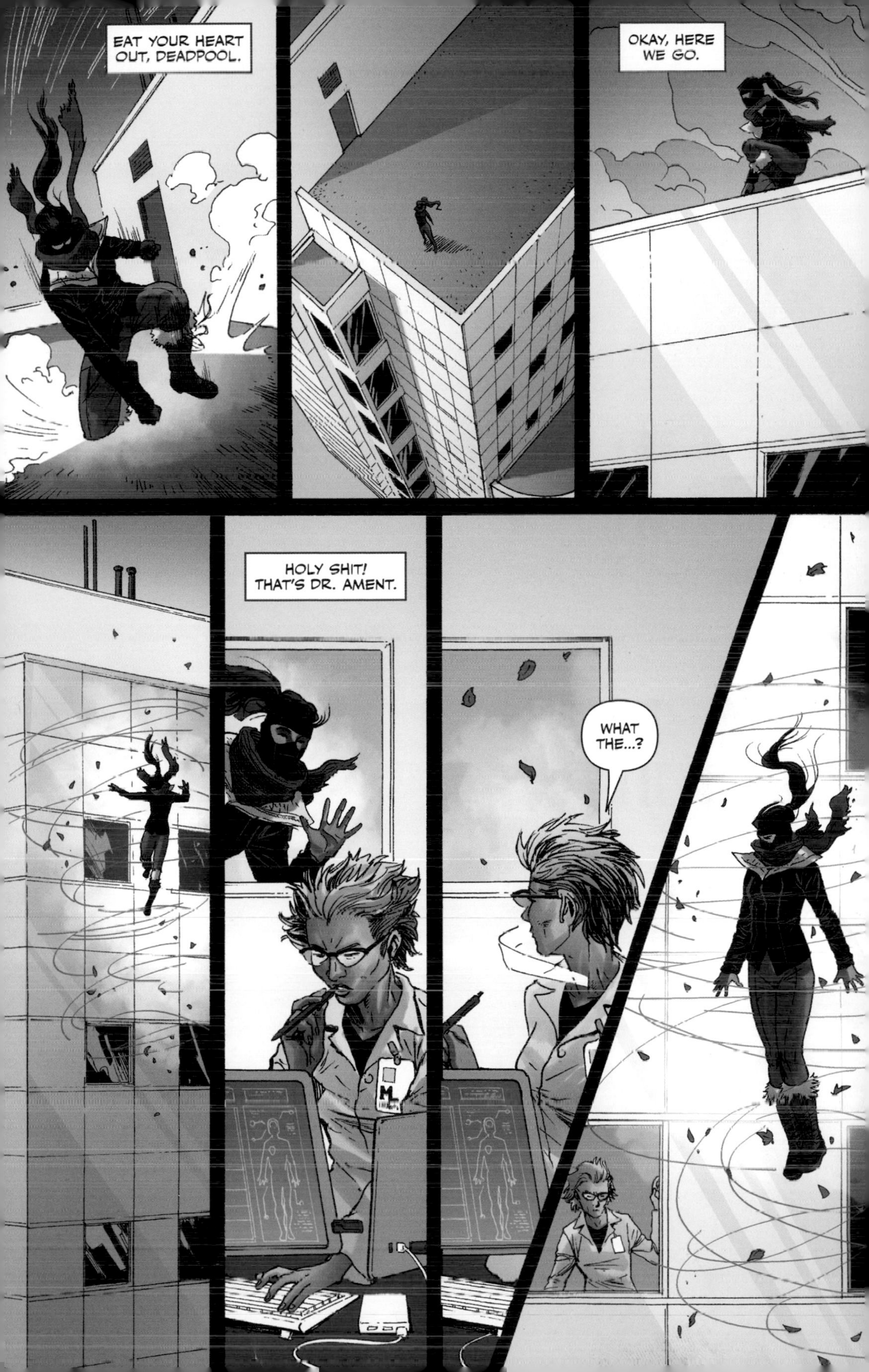
EAT YOUR HEART OUT, DEADPOOL.
OKAY, HERE WE GO.
HOLY SHIT! THAT'S DR. AMENT.
WHAT THE...?

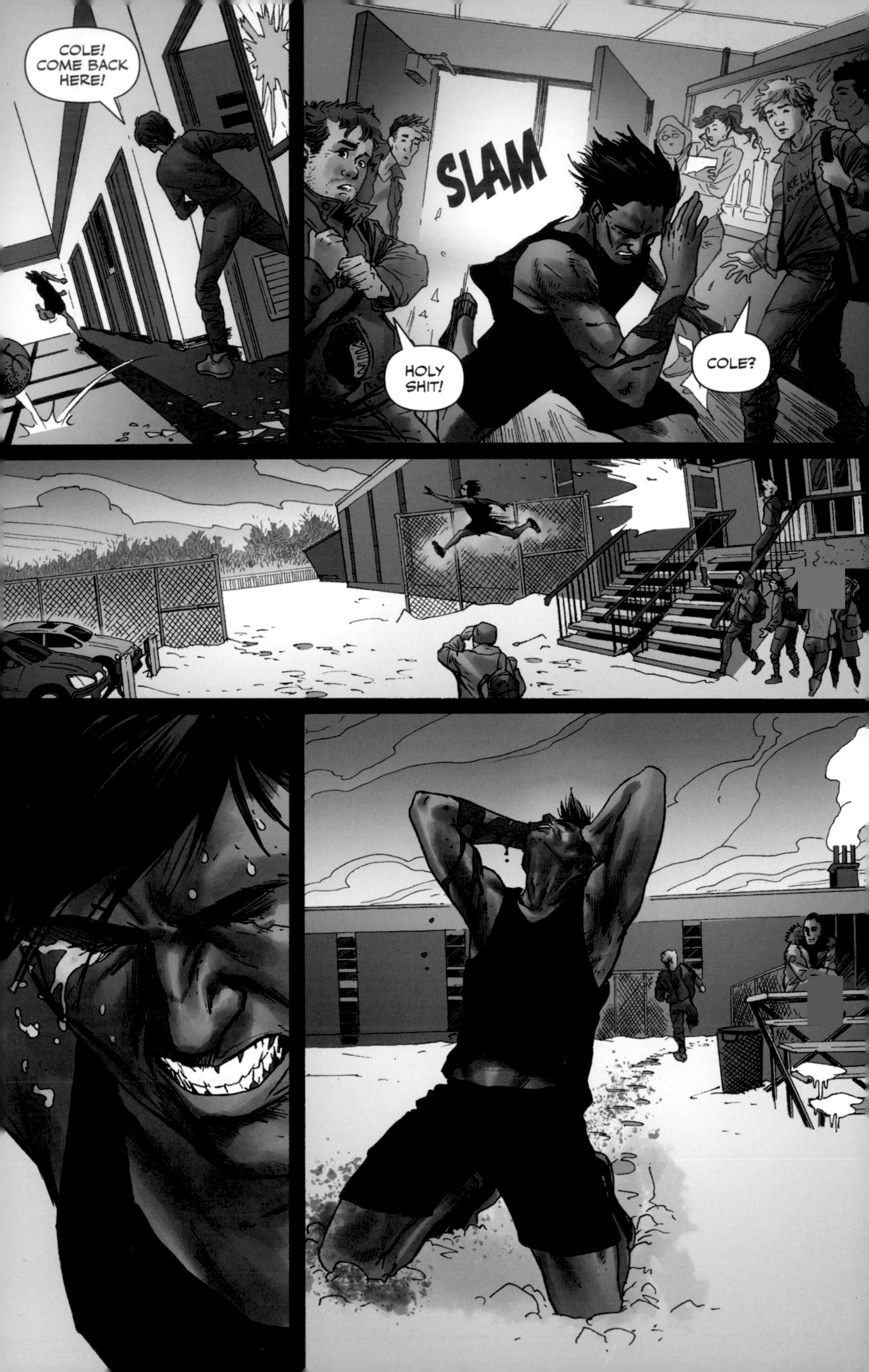
COLE! COME BACK HERE!
SLAM
HOLY SHIT!
COLE?

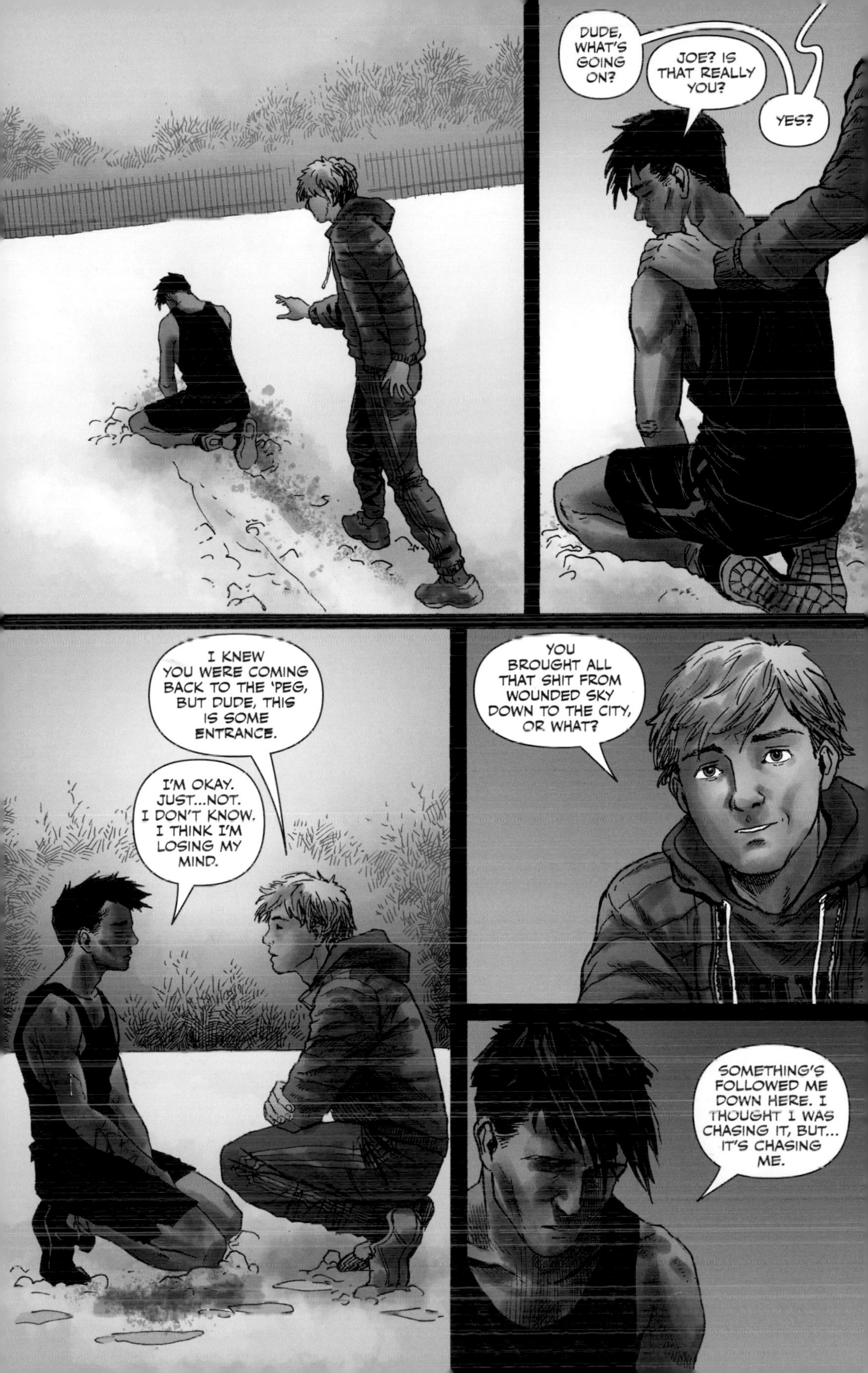
DUDE, WHAT'S GOING ON?
JOE? IS THAT REALLY YOU?
YES?
I KNEW YOU WERE COMING BACK TO THE 'PEG, BUT DUDE, THIS IS SOME ENTRANCE.
I'M OKAY. JUST...NOT. I DON'T KNOW. I THINK I'M LOSING MY MIND.
YOU BROUGHT ALL THAT SHIT FROM WOUNDED SKY DOWN TO THE CITY, OR WHAT?
SOMETHING'S FOLLOWED ME DOWN HERE. I THOUGHT I WAS CHASING IT, BUT... IT'S CHASING ME.

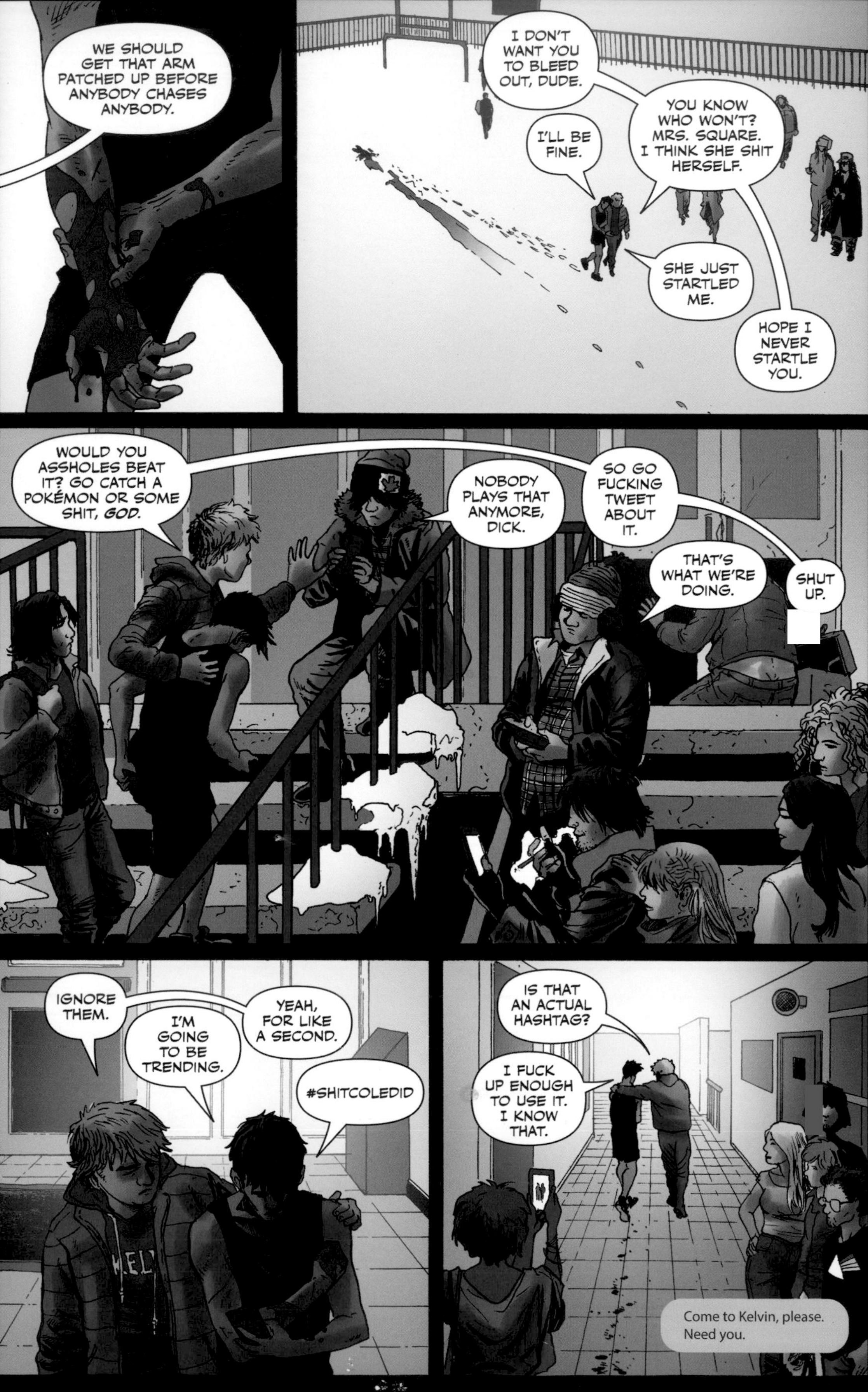
WE SHOULD GET THAT ARM PATCHED UP BEFORE ANYBODY CHASES ANYBODY.
I DON'T WANT YOU TO BLEED OUT, DUDE.
I'LL BE FINE.
YOU KNOW WHO WON'T? MRS. SQUARE. I THINK SHE SHIT HERSELF.
SHE JUST STARTLED ME.
HOPE I NEVER STARTLE YOU.
WOULD YOU ASSHOLES BEAT IT? GO CATCH A POKÉMON OR SOME SHIT, GOD.
NOBODY PLAYS THAT ANYMORE, DICK.
SO GO FUCKING TWEET ABOUT IT.
THAT'S WHAT WE'RE DOING.
SHUT UP.
IGNORE THEM.
I'M GOING TO BE TRENDING.
YEAH, FOR LIKE A SECOND.
#SHITCOLEDID
IS THAT AN ACTUAL HASHTAG?
I FUCK UP ENOUGH TO USE IT. I KNOW THAT.
Come to Kelvin, please. Need you.

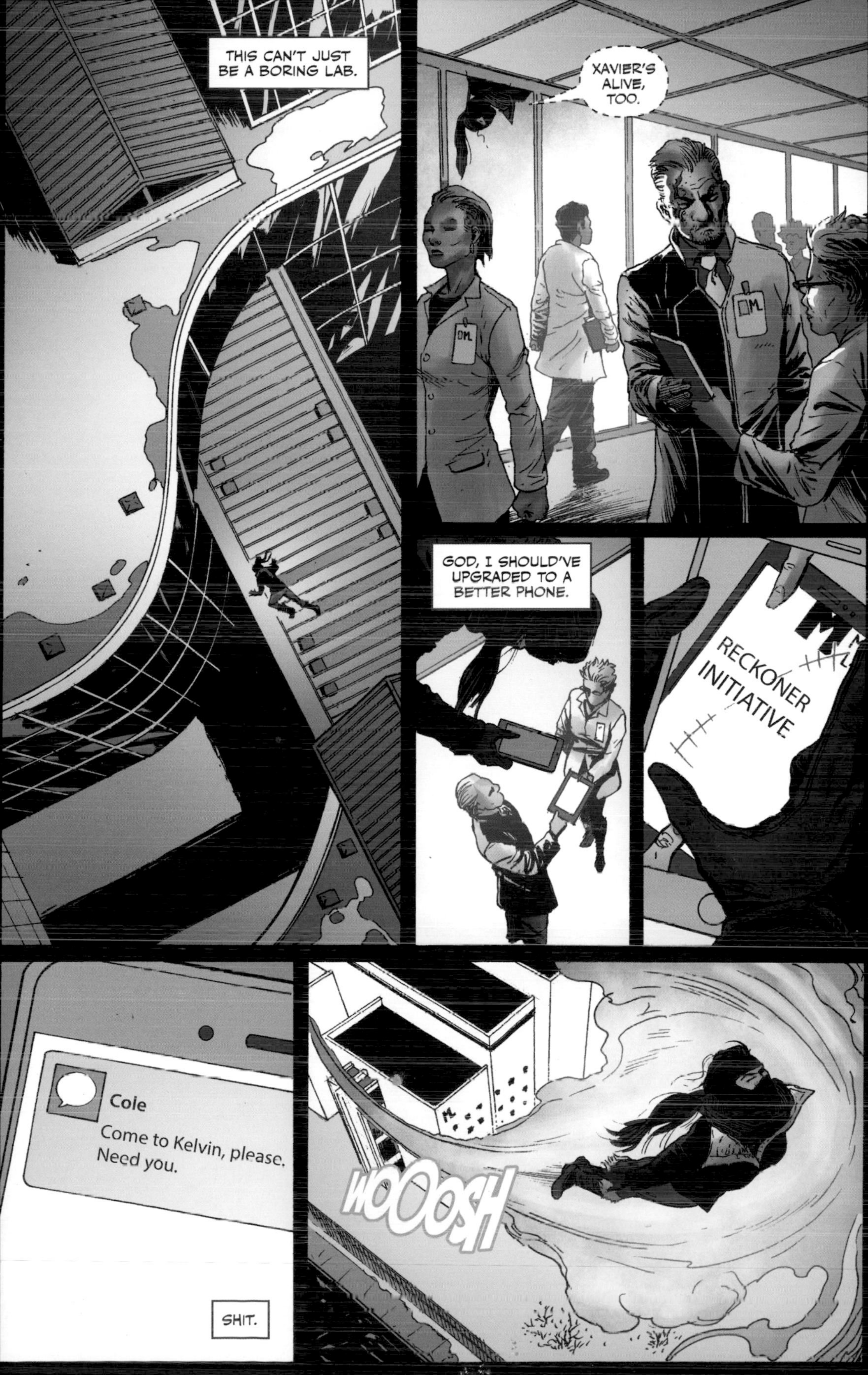
THIS CAN'T JUST BE A BORING LAB.
XAVIER'S ALIVE, TOO.
GOD, I SHOULD'VE UPGRADED TO A BETTER PHONE.
RECKONER INITIATIVE
Cole
Come to Kelvin, please. Need you.
SHIT.
WOOOSH

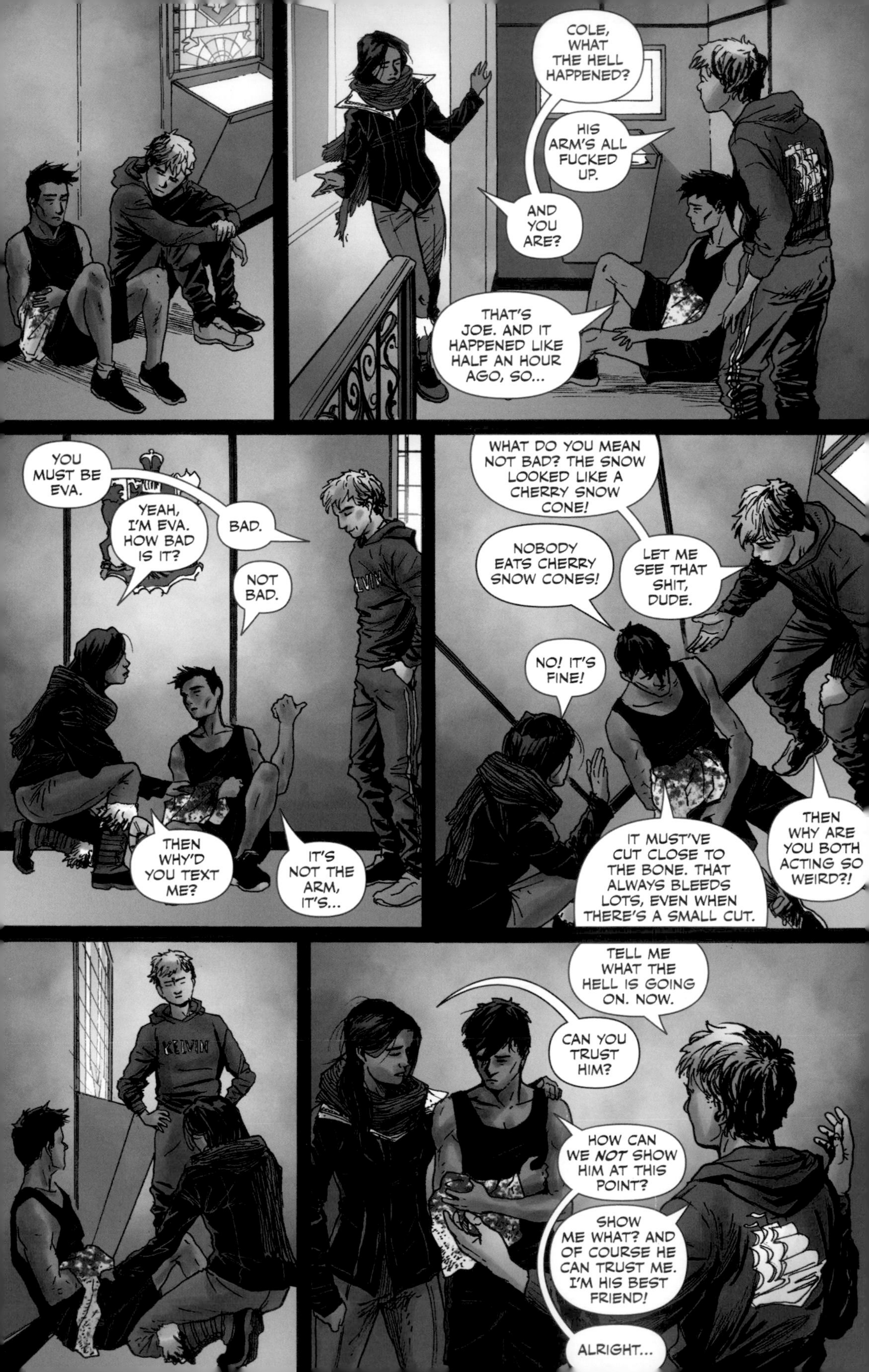
COLE, WHAT THE HELL HAPPENED?
HIS ARM'S ALL FUCKED UP.
AND YOU ARE?
THAT'S JOE. AND IT HAPPENED LIKE HALF AN HOUR AGO, SO...
YOU MUST BE EVA.
YEAH, I'M EVA. HOW BAD IS IT?
BAD.
NOT BAD.
THEN WHY'D YOU TEXT ME?
IT'S NOT THE ARM, IT'S...
WHAT DO YOU MEAN NOT BAD? THE SNOW LOOKED LIKE A CHERRY SNOW CONE!
NOBODY EATS CHERRY SNOW CONES!
LET ME SEE THAT SHIT, DUDE.
NO! IT'S FINE!
IT MUST'VE CUT CLOSE TO THE BONE. THAT ALWAYS BLEEDS LOTS, EVEN WHEN THERE'S A SMALL CUT.
THEN WHY ARE YOU BOTH ACTING SO WEIRD?!
TELL ME WHAT THE HELL IS GOING ON. NOW.
CAN YOU TRUST HIM?
HOW CAN WE NOT SHOW HIM AT THIS POINT?
SHOW ME WHAT? AND OF COURSE HE CAN TRUST ME. I'M HIS BEST FRIEND!
ALRIGHT...

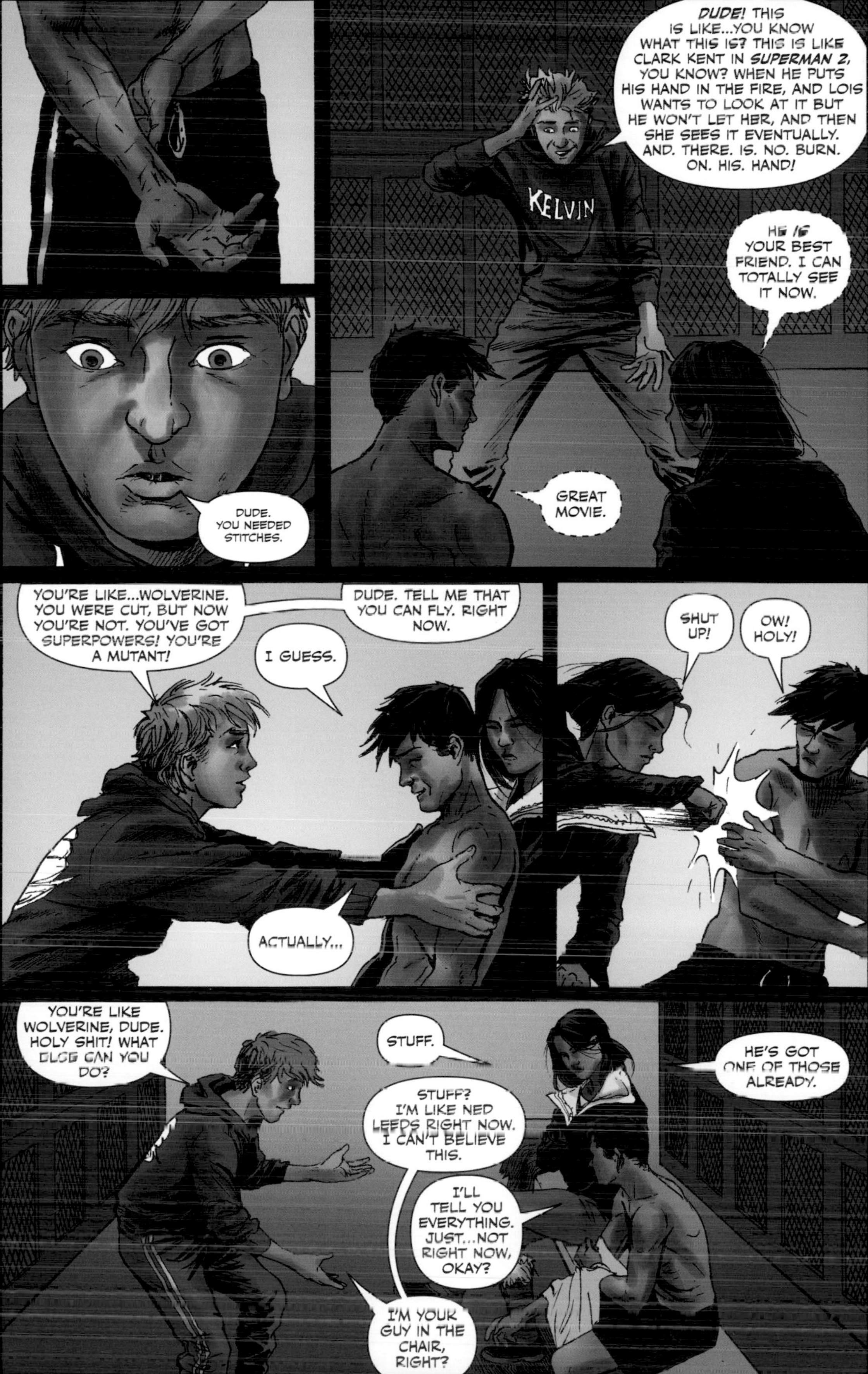
DUDE! THIS IS LIKE...YOU KNOW WHAT THIS IS? THIS IS LIKE CLARK KENT IN SUPERMAN 2, YOU KNOW? WHEN HE PUTS HIS HAND IN THE FIRE, AND LOIS WANTS TO LOOK AT IT BUT HE WON'T LET HER, AND THEN SHE SEES IT EVENTUALLY. AND. THERE. IS. NO. BURN. ON. HIS. HAND!
KELVIN
HE IS YOUR BEST FRIEND. I CAN TOTALLY SEE IT NOW.
DUDE. YOU NEEDED STITCHES.
GREAT MOVIE.
YOU'RE LIKE...WOLVERINE. YOU WERE CUT, BUT NOW YOU'RE NOT. YOU'VE GOT SUPERPOWERS! YOU'RE A MUTANT!
DUDE. TELL ME THAT YOU CAN FLY. RIGHT NOW.
I GUESS.
ACTUALLY...
SHUT UP!
OW! HOLY!
YOU'RE LIKE WOLVERINE, DUDE. HOLY SHIT! WHAT ELSE CAN YOU DO?
STUFF.
HE'S GOT ONE OF THOSE ALREADY.
STUFF? I'M LIKE NED LEEDS RIGHT NOW. I CAN'T BELIEVE THIS.
I'LL TELL YOU EVERYTHING. JUST...NOT RIGHT NOW, OKAY?
I'M YOUR GUY IN THE CHAIR, RIGHT?

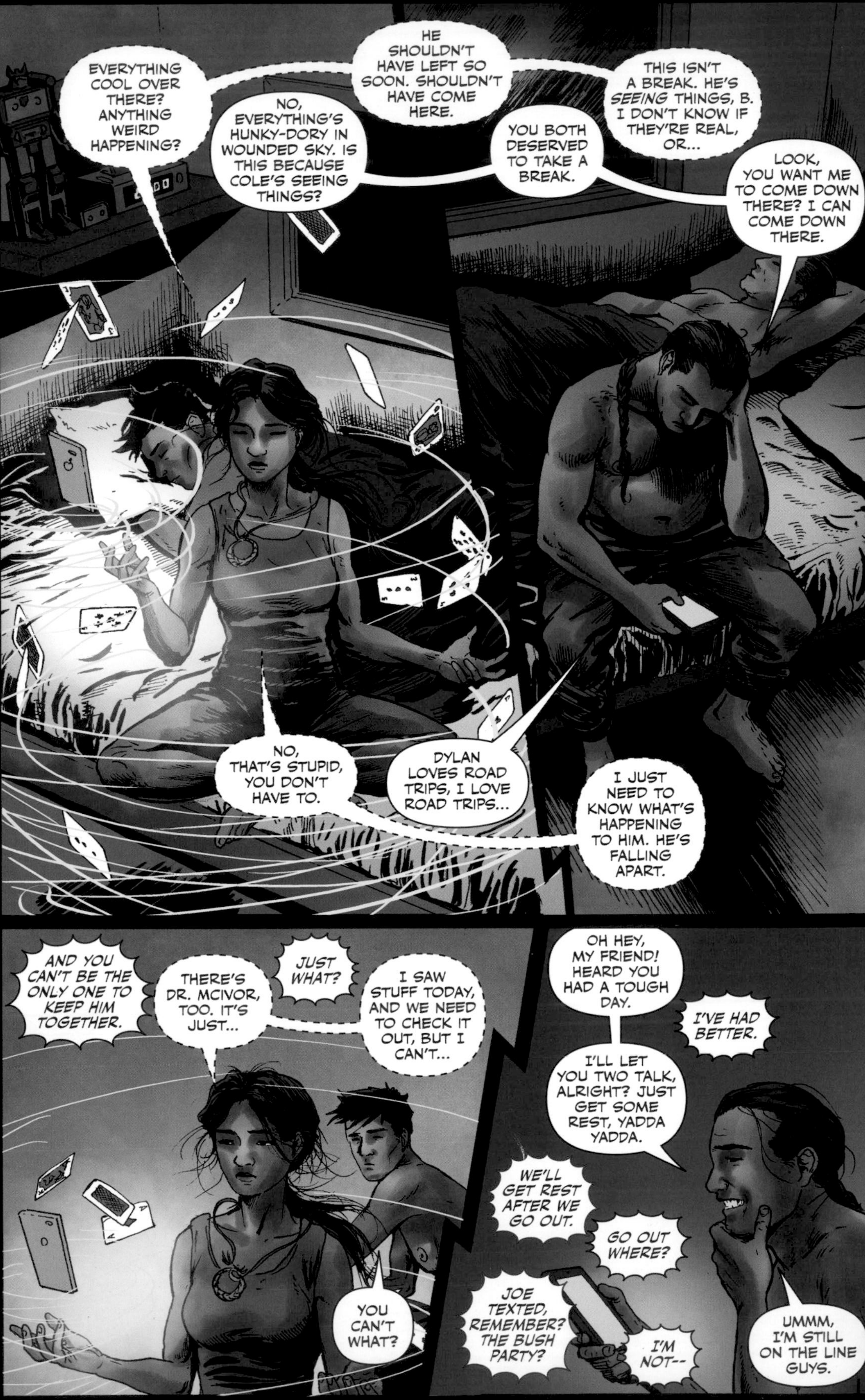
EVERYTHING COOL OVER THERE? ANYTHING WEIRD HAPPENING?
NO, EVERYTHING'S HUNKY-DORY IN WOUNDED SKY. IS THIS BECAUSE COLE'S SEEING THINGS?
HE SHOULDN'T HAVE LEFT SO SOON. SHOULDN'T HAVE COME HERE.
YOU BOTH DESERVED TO TAKE A BREAK.
THIS ISN'T A BREAK. HE'S *SEEING* THINGS, B. I DON'T KNOW IF THEY'RE REAL, OR...
LOOK, YOU WANT ME TO COME DOWN THERE? I CAN COME DOWN THERE.
NO, THAT'S STUPID, YOU DON'T HAVE TO.
DYLAN LOVES ROAD TRIPS, I LOVE ROAD TRIPS...
I JUST NEED TO KNOW WHAT'S HAPPENING TO HIM. HE'S FALLING APART.
AND YOU CAN'T BE THE ONLY ONE TO KEEP HIM TOGETHER.
THERE'S DR. MCIVOR, TOO. IT'S JUST...
JUST WHAT?
I SAW STUFF TODAY, AND WE NEED TO CHECK IT OUT, BUT I CAN'T...
YOU CAN'T WHAT?
OH HEY, MY FRIEND! HEARD YOU HAD A TOUGH DAY.
I'VE HAD BETTER.
I'LL LET YOU TWO TALK, ALRIGHT? JUST GET SOME REST, YADDA YADDA.
WE'LL GET REST AFTER WE GO OUT.
GO OUT WHERE?
JOE TEXTED, REMEMBER? THE BUSH PARTY?
I'M NOT--
UMMM, I'M STILL ON THE LINE GUYS.

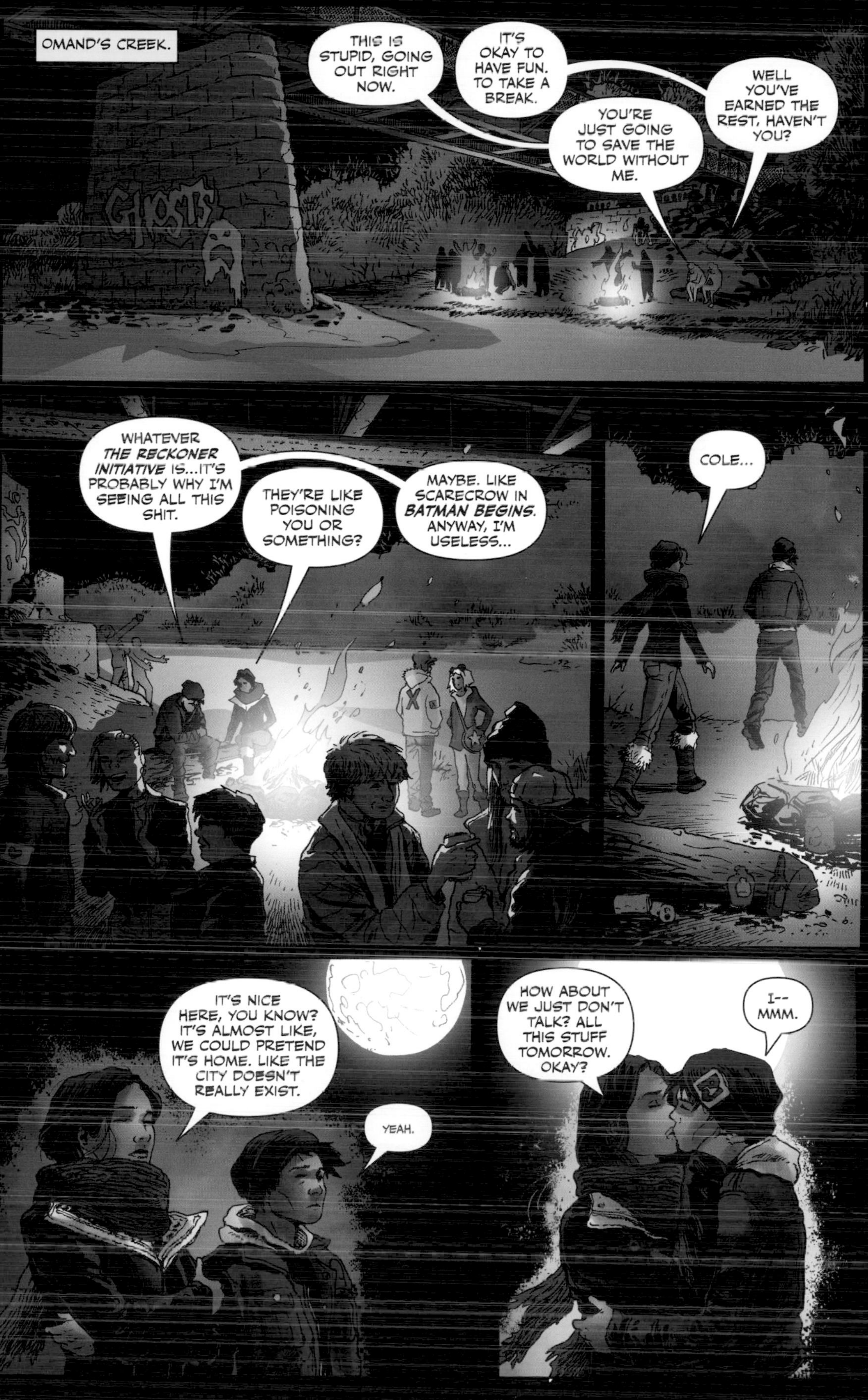

OMAND'S CREEK.
THIS IS STUPID, GOING OUT RIGHT NOW.
IT'S OKAY TO HAVE FUN. TO TAKE A BREAK.
YOU'RE JUST GOING TO SAVE THE WORLD WITHOUT ME.
WELL YOU'VE EARNED THE REST, HAVEN'T YOU?
WHATEVER *THE RECKONER INITIATIVE* IS...IT'S PROBABLY WHY I'M SEEING ALL THIS SHIT.
THEY'RE LIKE POISONING YOU OR SOMETHING?
MAYBE. LIKE SCARECROW IN *BATMAN BEGINS*. ANYWAY, I'M USELESS...
COLE...
IT'S NICE HERE, YOU KNOW? IT'S ALMOST LIKE, WE COULD PRETEND IT'S HOME. LIKE THE CITY DOESN'T REALLY EXIST.
YEAH.
HOW ABOUT WE JUST DON'T TALK? ALL THIS STUFF TOMORROW. OKAY?
I-- MMM.

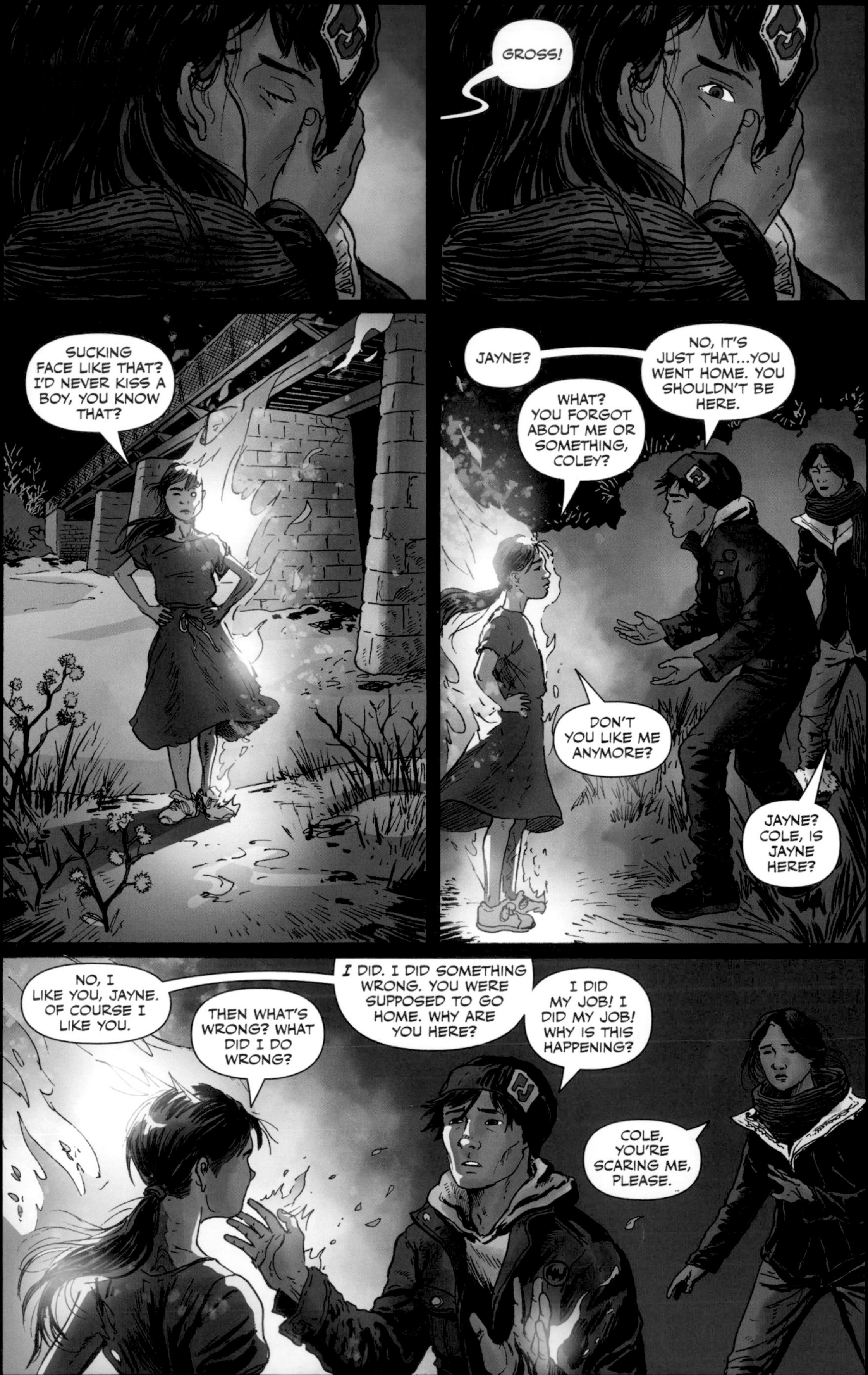
GROSS!
SUCKING FACE LIKE THAT? I'D NEVER KISS A BOY, YOU KNOW THAT?
JAYNE?
NO, IT'S JUST THAT...YOU WENT HOME. YOU SHOULDN'T BE HERE.
WHAT? YOU FORGOT ABOUT ME OR SOMETHING, COLEY?
DON'T YOU LIKE ME ANYMORE?
JAYNE? COLE, IS JAYNE HERE?
NO, I LIKE YOU, JAYNE. OF COURSE I LIKE YOU.
THEN WHAT'S WRONG? WHAT DID I DO WRONG?
I DID. I DID SOMETHING WRONG. YOU WERE SUPPOSED TO GO HOME. WHY ARE YOU HERE?
I DID MY JOB! I DID MY JOB! WHY IS THIS HAPPENING?
COLE, YOU'RE SCARING ME, PLEASE.

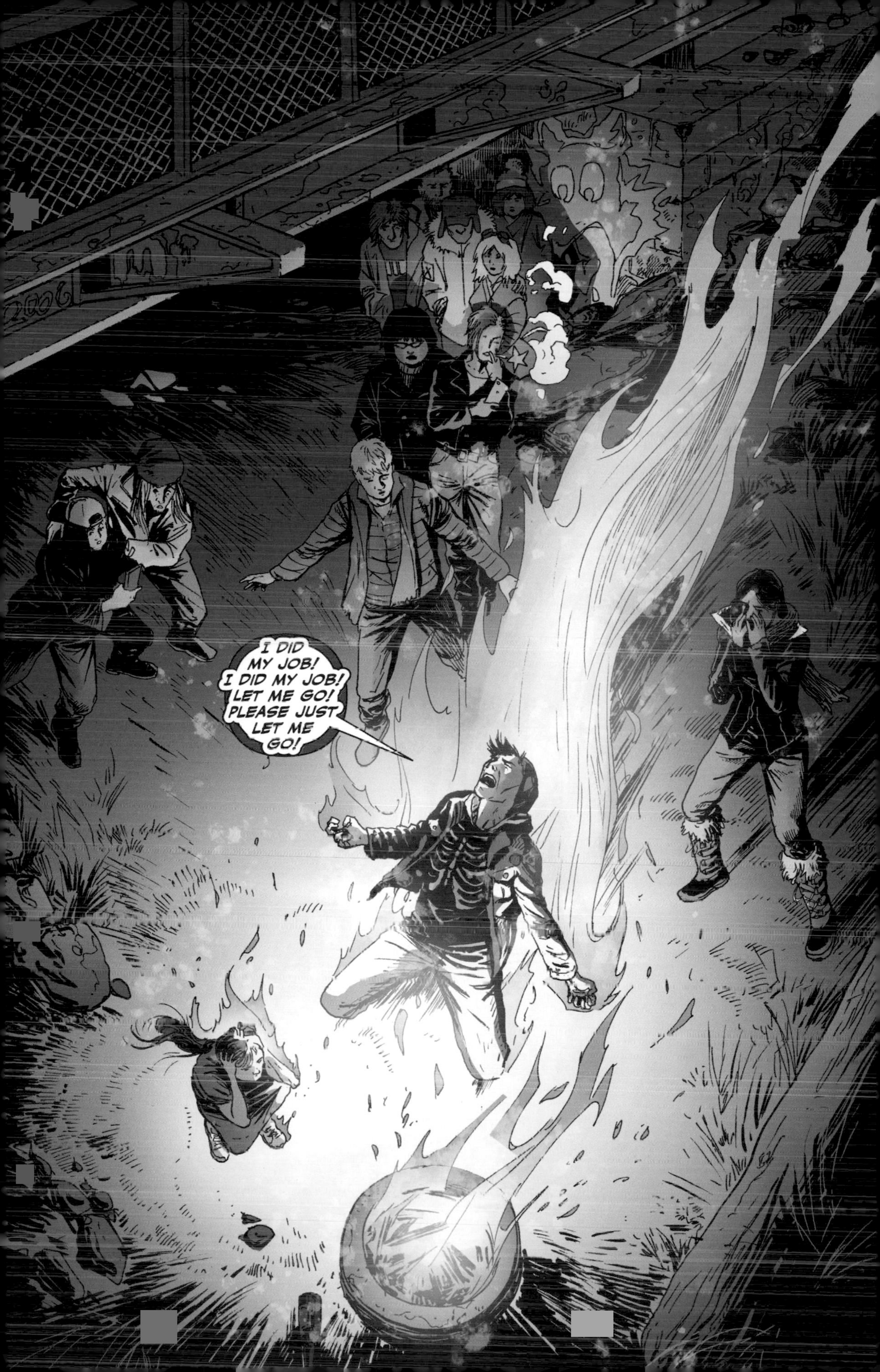
I DID MY JOB! I DID MY JOB! LET ME GO! PLEASE JUST LET ME GO!

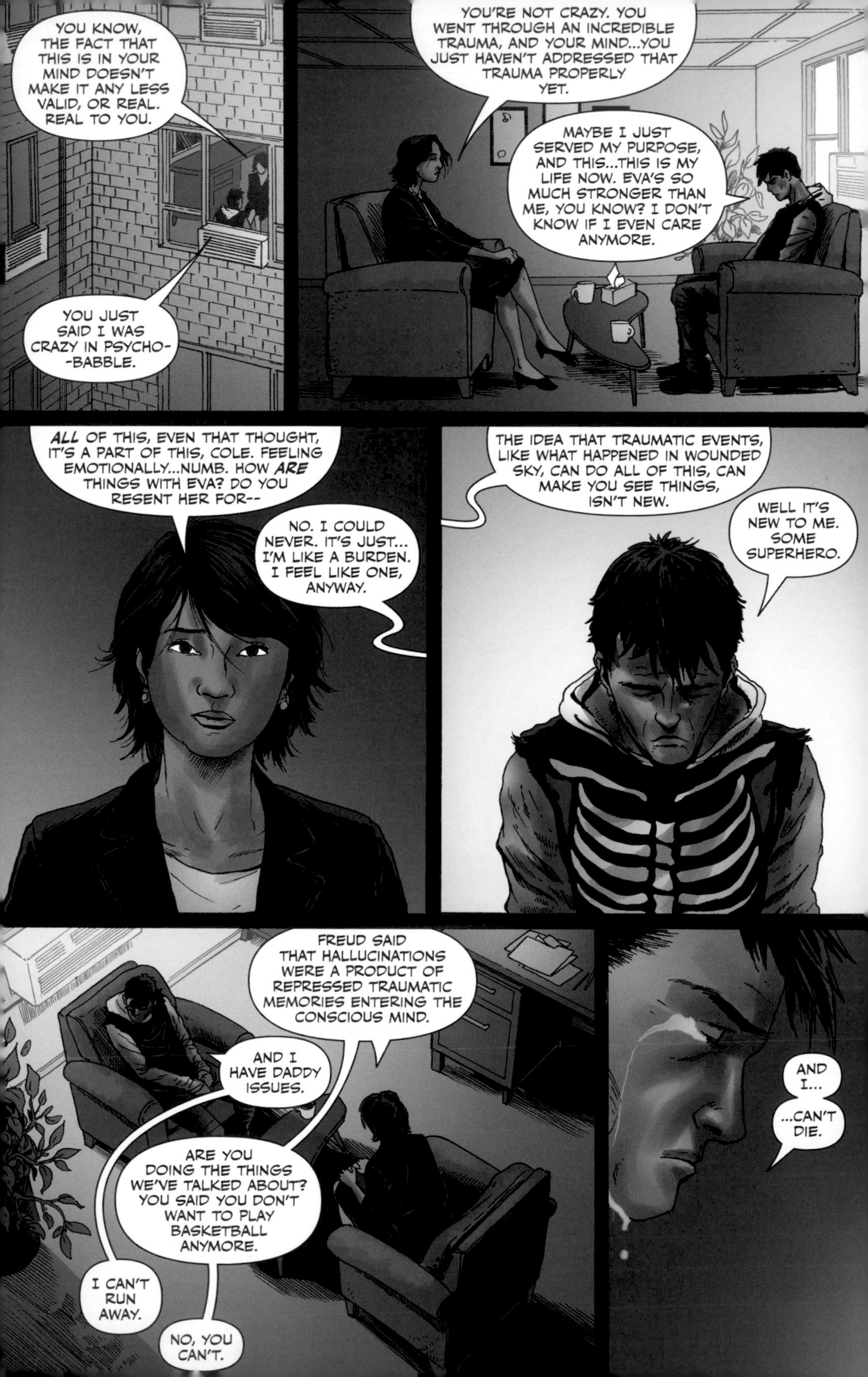
YOU KNOW, THE FACT THAT THIS IS IN YOUR MIND DOESN'T MAKE IT ANY LESS VALID, OR REAL. REAL TO YOU.
YOU JUST SAID I WAS CRAZY IN PSYCHO-BABBLE.
YOU'RE NOT CRAZY. YOU WENT THROUGH AN INCREDIBLE TRAUMA, AND YOUR MIND...YOU JUST HAVEN'T ADDRESSED THAT TRAUMA PROPERLY YET.
MAYBE I JUST SERVED MY PURPOSE, AND THIS...THIS IS MY LIFE NOW. EVA'S SO MUCH STRONGER THAN ME, YOU KNOW? I DON'T KNOW IF I EVEN CARE ANYMORE.
ALL OF THIS, EVEN THAT THOUGHT, IT'S A PART OF THIS, COLE. FEELING EMOTIONALLY...NUMB. HOW *ARE* THINGS WITH EVA? DO YOU RESENT HER FOR--
NO. I COULD NEVER. IT'S JUST... I'M LIKE A BURDEN. I FEEL LIKE ONE, ANYWAY.
THE IDEA THAT TRAUMATIC EVENTS, LIKE WHAT HAPPENED IN WOUNDED SKY, CAN DO ALL OF THIS, CAN MAKE YOU SEE THINGS, ISN'T NEW.
WELL IT'S NEW TO ME. SOME SUPERHERO.
FREUD SAID THAT HALLUCINATIONS WERE A PRODUCT OF REPRESSED TRAUMATIC MEMORIES ENTERING THE CONSCIOUS MIND.
AND I HAVE DADDY ISSUES.
ARE YOU DOING THE THINGS WE'VE TALKED ABOUT? YOU SAID YOU DON'T WANT TO PLAY BASKETBALL ANYMORE.
I CAN'T RUN AWAY.
NO, YOU CAN'T.
AND I...
...CAN'T DIE.

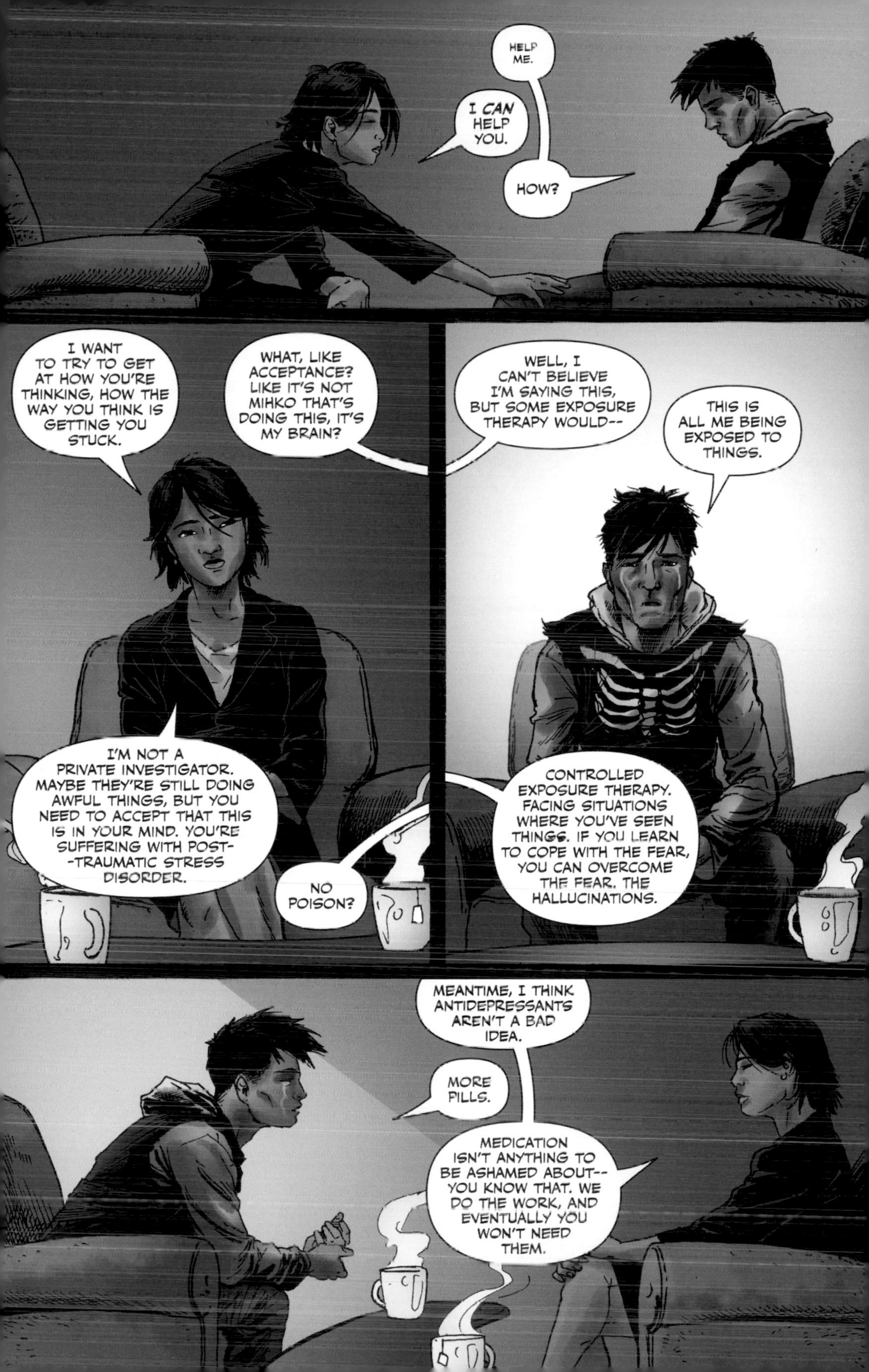
HELP ME.
I CAN HELP YOU.
HOW?
I WANT TO TRY TO GET AT HOW YOU'RE THINKING, HOW THE WAY YOU THINK IS GETTING YOU STUCK.
WHAT, LIKE ACCEPTANCE? LIKE IT'S NOT MIHKO THAT'S DOING THIS, IT'S MY BRAIN?
I'M NOT A PRIVATE INVESTIGATOR. MAYBE THEY'RE STILL DOING AWFUL THINGS, BUT YOU NEED TO ACCEPT THAT THIS IS IN YOUR MIND. YOU'RE SUFFERING WITH POST--TRAUMATIC STRESS DISORDER.
NO POISON?
WELL, I CAN'T BELIEVE I'M SAYING THIS, BUT SOME EXPOSURE THERAPY WOULD--
THIS IS ALL ME BEING EXPOSED TO THINGS.
CONTROLLED EXPOSURE THERAPY. FACING SITUATIONS WHERE YOU'VE SEEN THINGS. IF YOU LEARN TO COPE WITH THE FEAR, YOU CAN OVERCOME THE FEAR. THE HALLUCINATIONS.
MEANTIME, I THINK ANTIDEPRESSANTS AREN'T A BAD IDEA.
MORE PILLS.
MEDICATION ISN'T ANYTHING TO BE ASHAMED ABOUT-- YOU KNOW THAT. WE DO THE WORK, AND EVENTUALLY YOU WON'T NEED THEM.

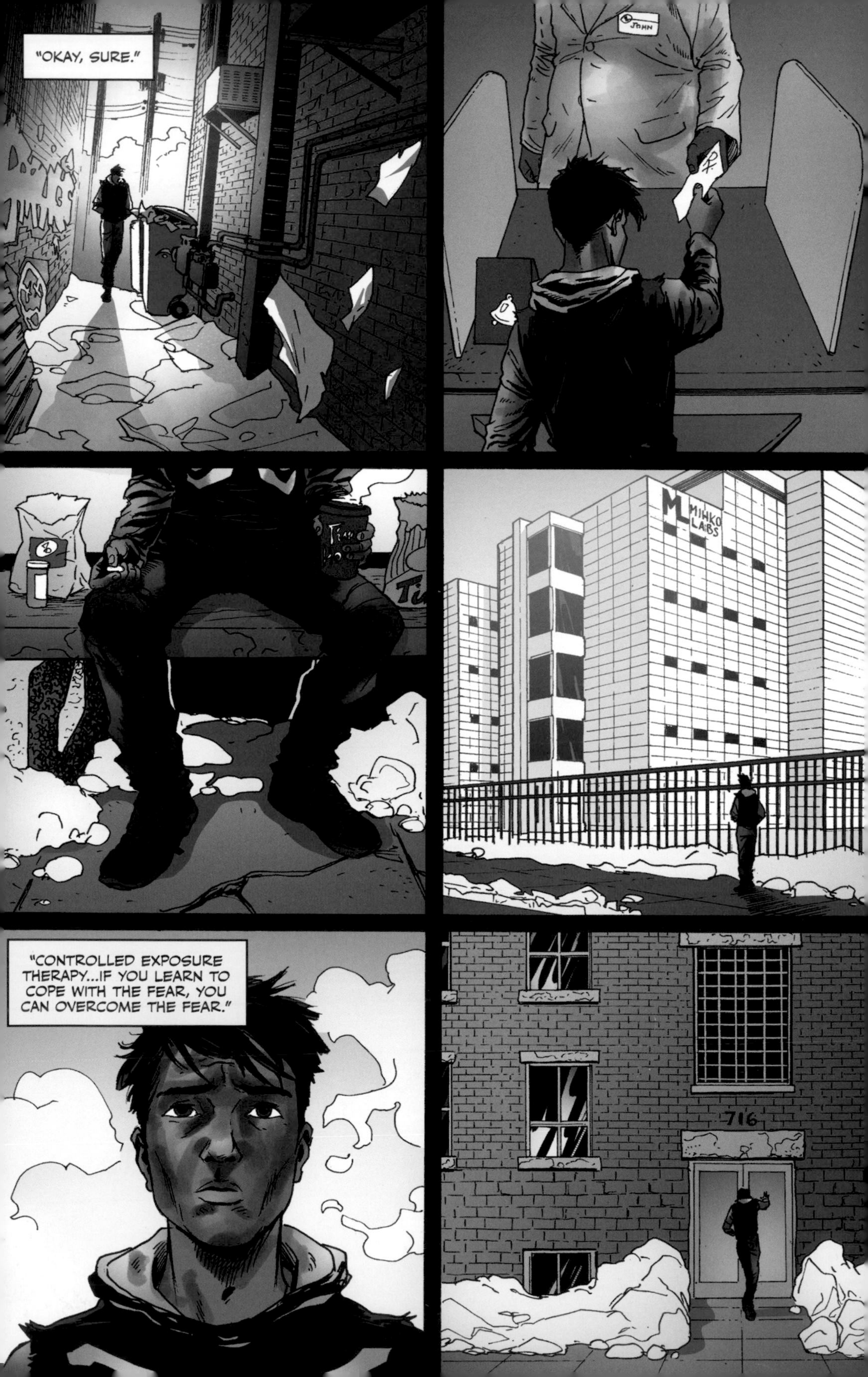
"OKAY, SURE."
JOHN
MIHKO LABS
"CONTROLLED EXPOSURE THERAPY...IF YOU LEARN TO COPE WITH THE FEAR, YOU CAN OVERCOME THE FEAR."
716

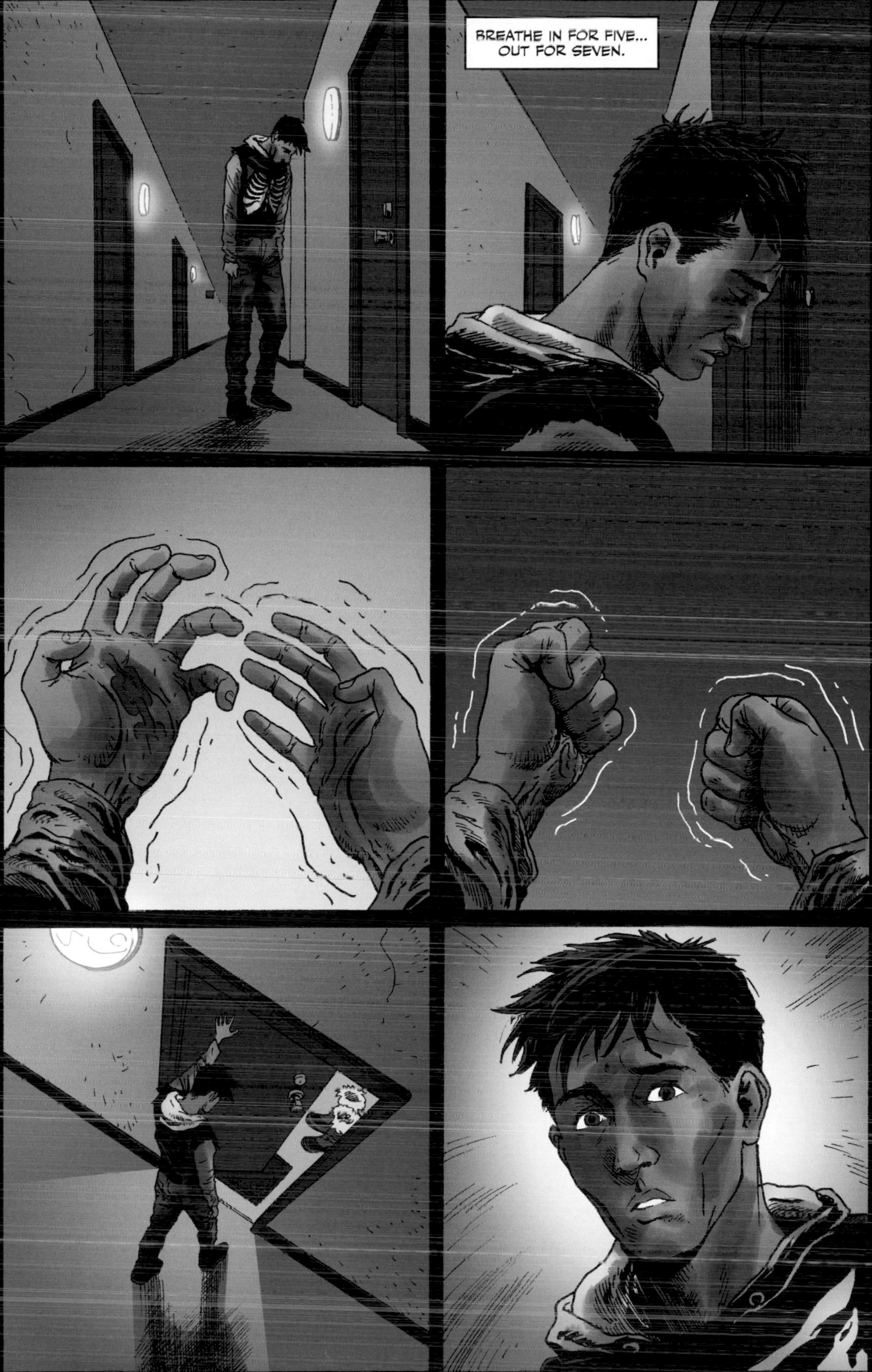
BREATHE IN FOR FIVE...
OUT FOR SEVEN.

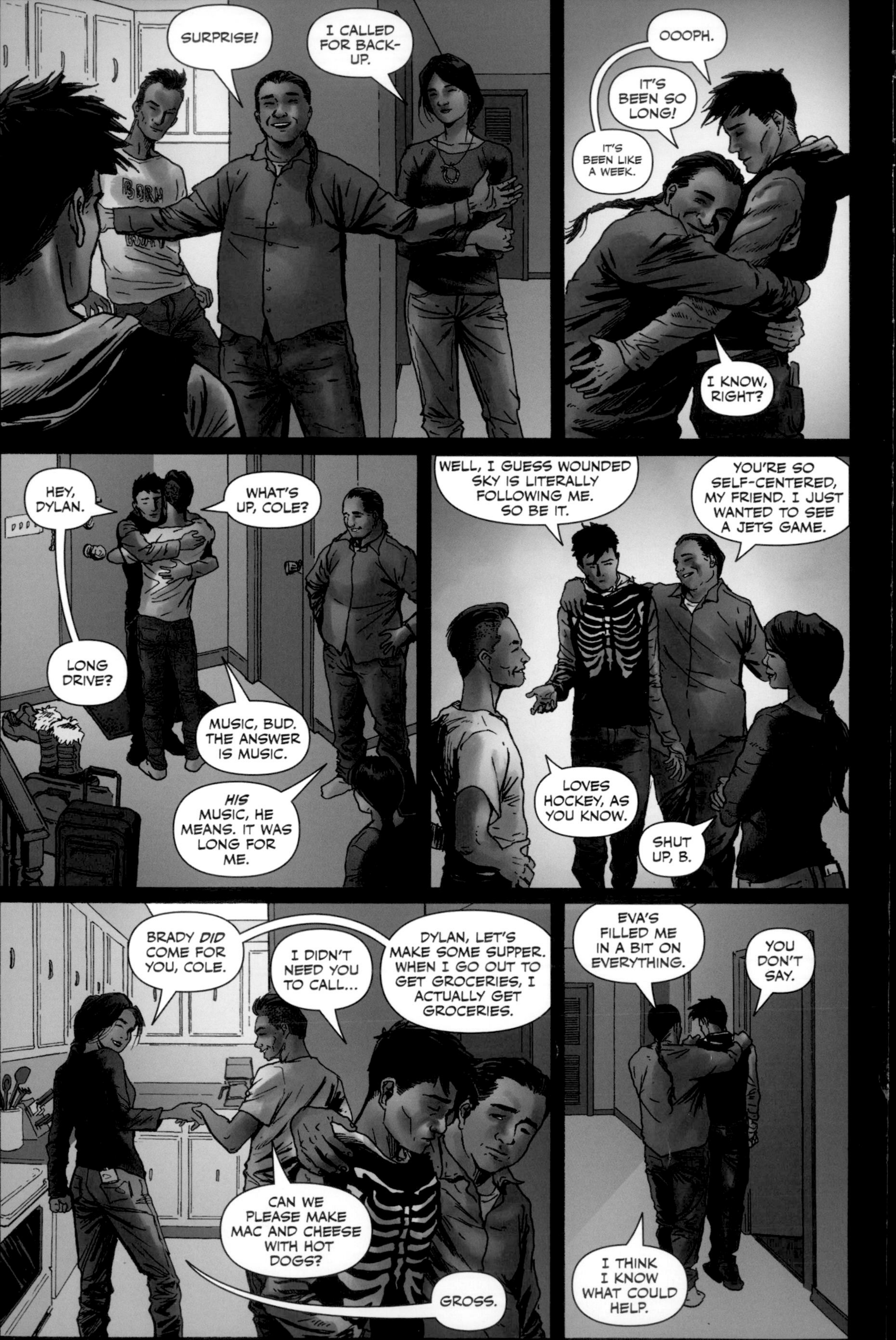
SURPRISE!
I CALLED FOR BACK-UP.
OOOPH.
IT'S BEEN SO LONG!
IT'S BEEN LIKE A WEEK.
I KNOW, RIGHT?
HEY, DYLAN.
WHAT'S UP, COLE?
LONG DRIVE?
MUSIC, BUD. THE ANSWER IS MUSIC.
HIS MUSIC, HE MEANS. IT WAS LONG FOR ME.
WELL, I GUESS WOUNDED SKY IS LITERALLY FOLLOWING ME. SO BE IT.
YOU'RE SO SELF-CENTERED, MY FRIEND. I JUST WANTED TO SEE A JETS GAME.
LOVES HOCKEY, AS YOU KNOW.
SHUT UP, B.
BRADY *DID* COME FOR YOU, COLE.
I DIDN'T NEED YOU TO CALL...
DYLAN, LET'S MAKE SOME SUPPER. WHEN I GO OUT TO GET GROCERIES, I ACTUALLY GET GROCERIES.
CAN WE PLEASE MAKE MAC AND CHEESE WITH HOT DOGS?
GROSS.
EVA'S FILLED ME IN A BIT ON EVERYTHING.
YOU DON'T SAY.
I THINK I KNOW WHAT COULD HELP.

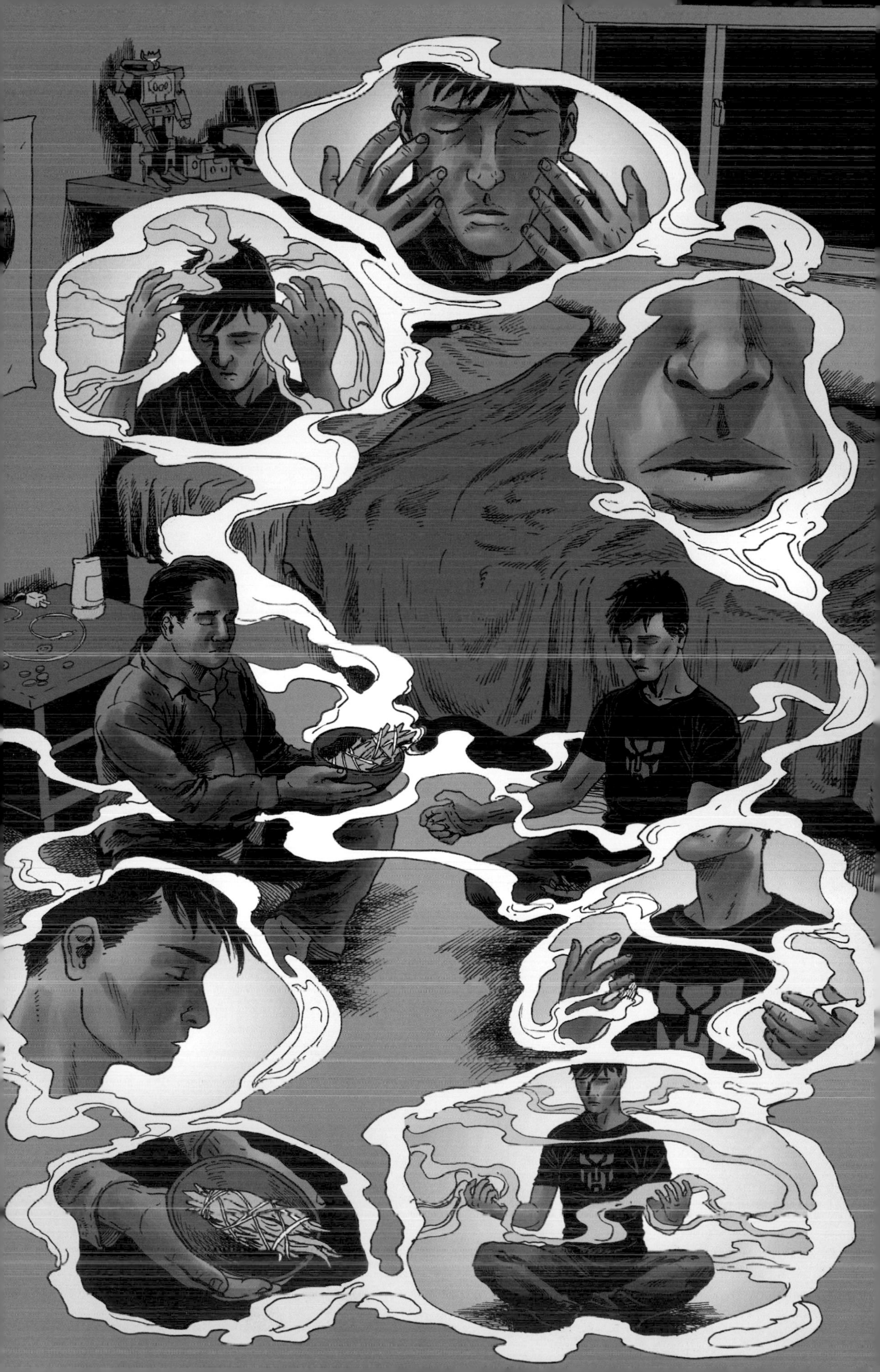

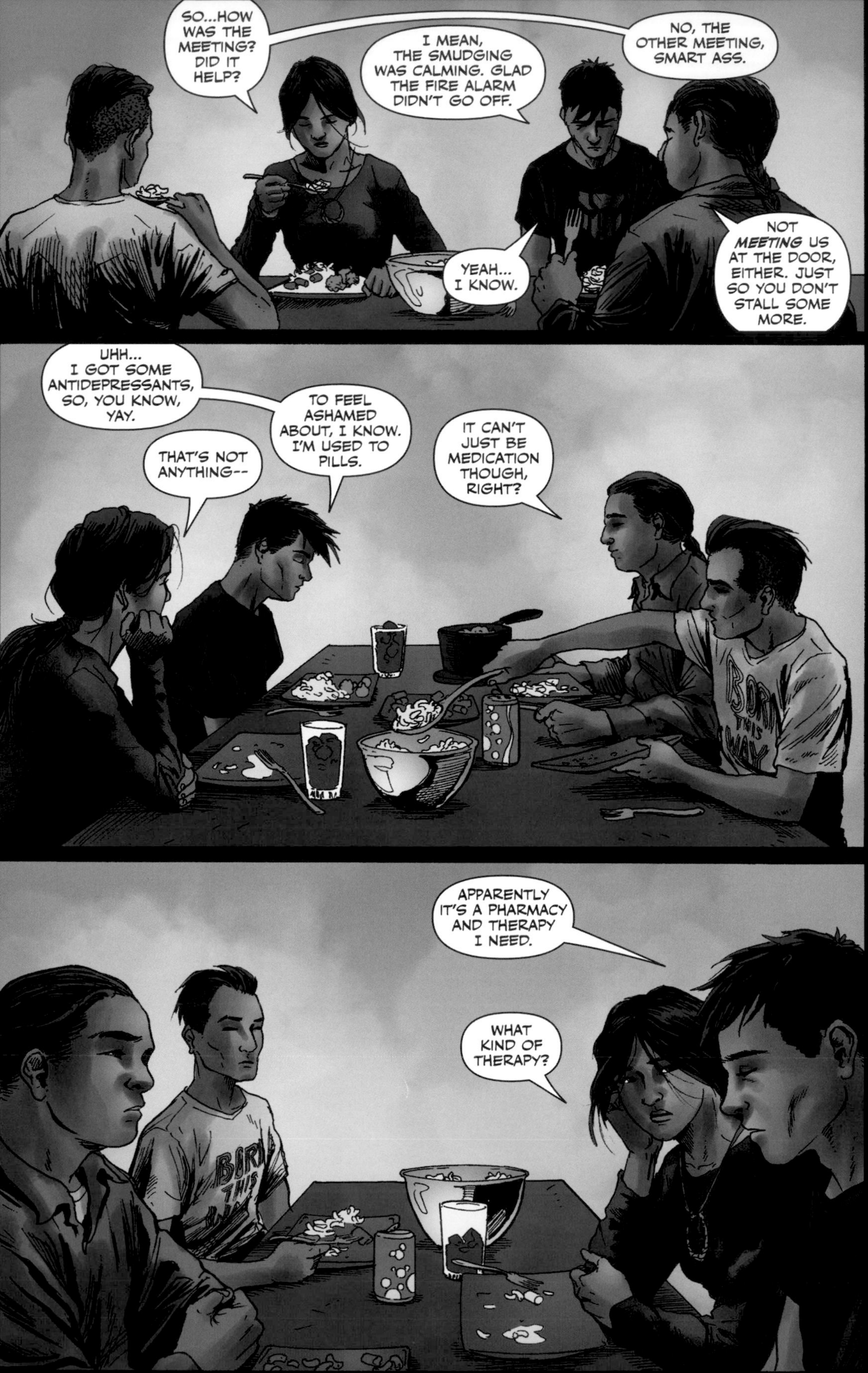
SO...HOW WAS THE MEETING? DID IT HELP?
I MEAN, THE SMUDGING WAS CALMING. GLAD THE FIRE ALARM DIDN'T GO OFF.
NO, THE OTHER MEETING, SMART ASS.
YEAH... I KNOW.
NOT *MEETING* US AT THE DOOR, EITHER. JUST SO YOU DON'T STALL SOME MORE.
UHH... I GOT SOME ANTIDEPRESSANTS, SO, YOU KNOW, YAY.
THAT'S NOT ANYTHING--
TO FEEL ASHAMED ABOUT, I KNOW. I'M USED TO PILLS.
IT CAN'T JUST BE MEDICATION THOUGH, RIGHT?
APPARENTLY IT'S A PHARMACY AND THERAPY I NEED.
WHAT KIND OF THERAPY?

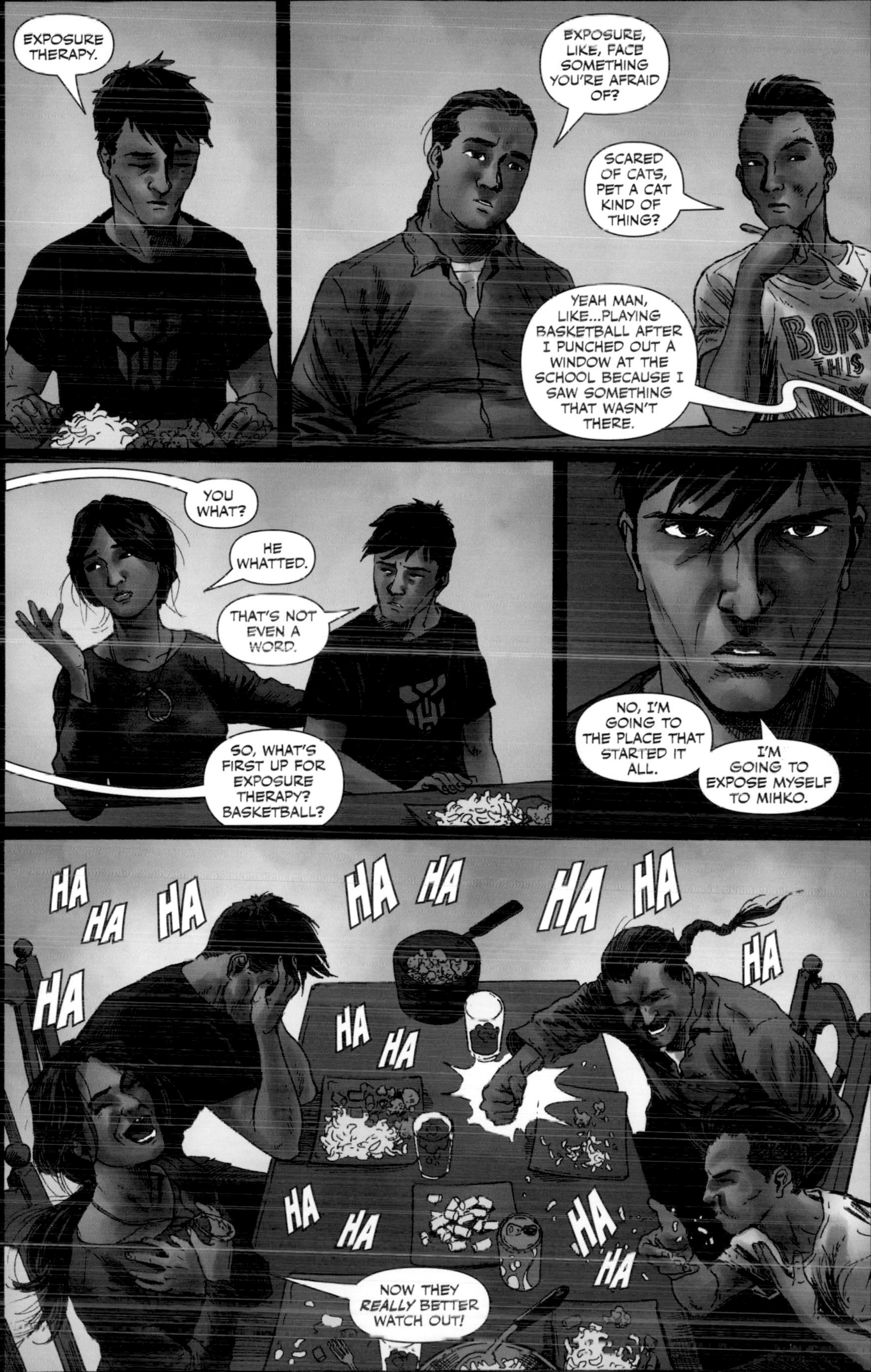
EXPOSURE THERAPY.
EXPOSURE, LIKE, FACE SOMETHING YOU'RE AFRAID OF?
SCARED OF CATS, PET A CAT KIND OF THING?
YEAH MAN, LIKE...PLAYING BASKETBALL AFTER I PUNCHED OUT A WINDOW AT THE SCHOOL BECAUSE I SAW SOMETHING THAT WASN'T THERE.
YOU WHAT?
HE WHATTED.
THAT'S NOT EVEN A WORD.
SO, WHAT'S FIRST UP FOR EXPOSURE THERAPY? BASKETBALL?
NO, I'M GOING TO THE PLACE THAT STARTED IT ALL.
I'M GOING TO EXPOSE MYSELF TO MIHKO.
HA HA HA HA HA HA HA HA HA HA HA HA HA HA HA HA HA
NOW THEY *REALLY* BETTER WATCH OUT!

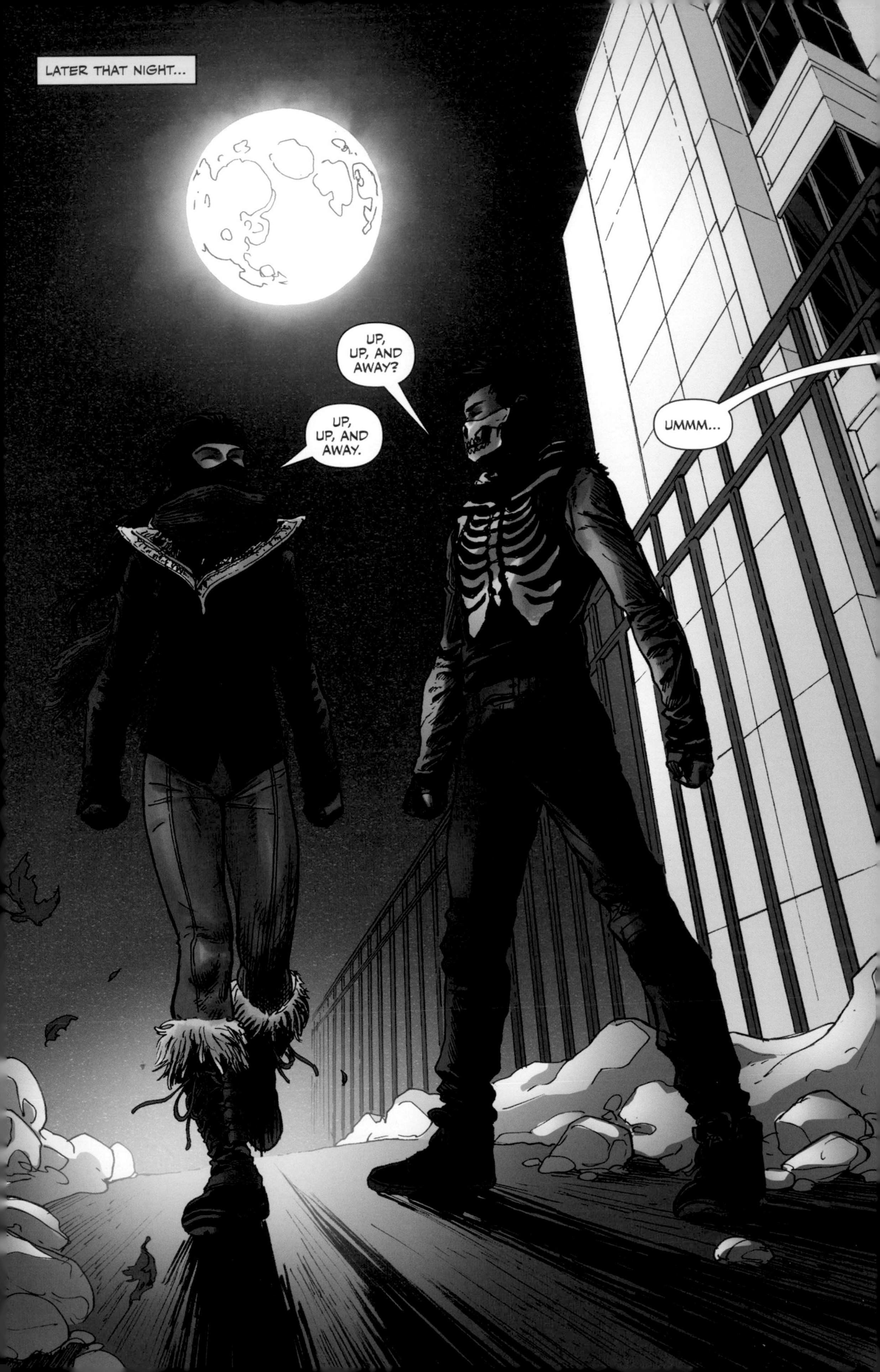
LATER THAT NIGHT...
UP, UP, AND AWAY?
UP, UP, AND AWAY.
UMMM...

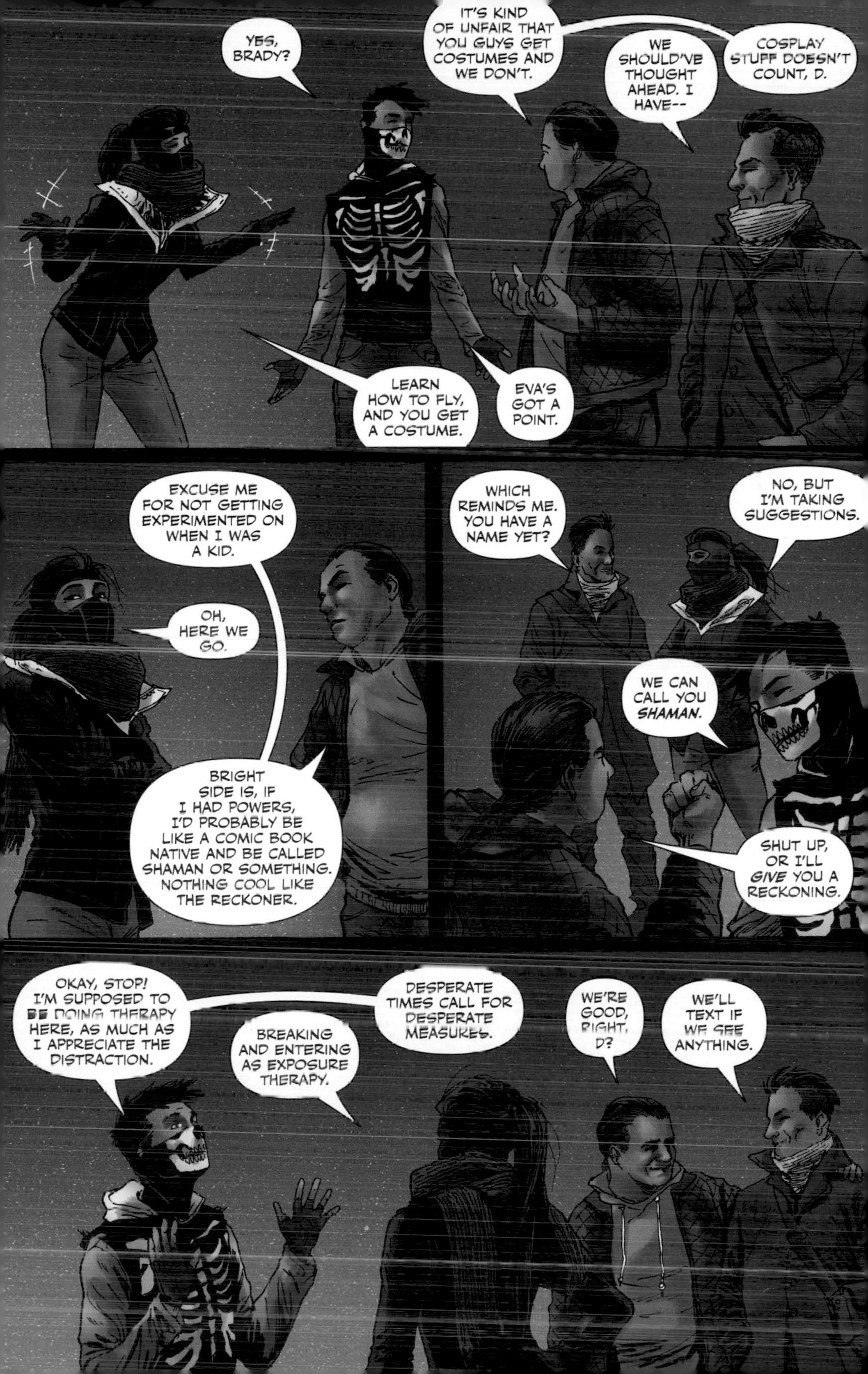
YES, BRADY?
IT'S KIND OF UNFAIR THAT YOU GUYS GET COSTUMES AND WE DON'T.
COSPLAY STUFF DOESN'T COUNT, D.
WE SHOULD'VE THOUGHT AHEAD. I HAVE--
LEARN HOW TO FLY, AND YOU GET A COSTUME.
EVA'S GOT A POINT.
EXCUSE ME FOR NOT GETTING EXPERIMENTED ON WHEN I WAS A KID.
OH, HERE WE GO.
BRIGHT SIDE IS, IF I HAD POWERS, I'D PROBABLY BE LIKE A COMIC BOOK NATIVE AND BE CALLED SHAMAN OR SOMETHING. NOTHING COOL LIKE THE RECKONER.
WHICH REMINDS ME. YOU HAVE A NAME YET?
NO, BUT I'M TAKING SUGGESTIONS.
WE CAN CALL YOU *SHAMAN*.
SHUT UP, OR I'LL *GIVE* YOU A RECKONING.
OKAY, STOP! I'M SUPPOSED TO BE DOING THERAPY HERE, AS MUCH AS I APPRECIATE THE DISTRACTION.
BREAKING AND ENTERING AS EXPOSURE THERAPY.
DESPERATE TIMES CALL FOR DESPERATE MEASURES.
WE'RE GOOD, RIGHT, D?
WE'LL TEXT IF WE SEE ANYTHING.

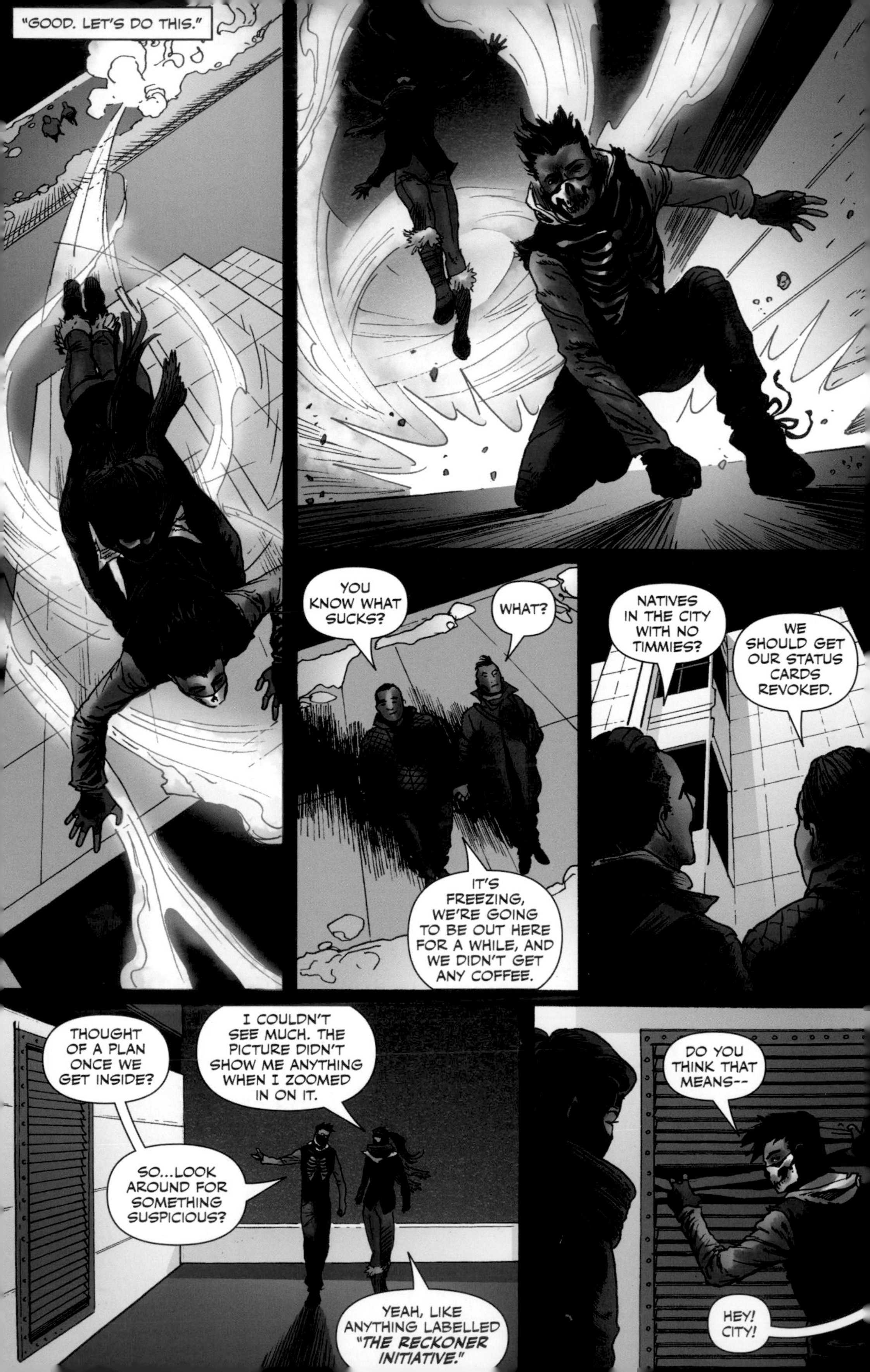
"GOOD. LET'S DO THIS."
YOU KNOW WHAT SUCKS?
WHAT?
IT'S FREEZING, WE'RE GOING TO BE OUT HERE FOR A WHILE, AND WE DIDN'T GET ANY COFFEE.
NATIVES IN THE CITY WITH NO TIMMIES?
WE SHOULD GET OUR STATUS CARDS REVOKED.
THOUGHT OF A PLAN ONCE WE GET INSIDE?
I COULDN'T SEE MUCH. THE PICTURE DIDN'T SHOW ME ANYTHING WHEN I ZOOMED IN ON IT.
SO...LOOK AROUND FOR SOMETHING SUSPICIOUS?
YEAH, LIKE ANYTHING LABELLED "*THE RECKONER INITIATIVE.*"
DO YOU THINK THAT MEANS--
HEY! CITY!

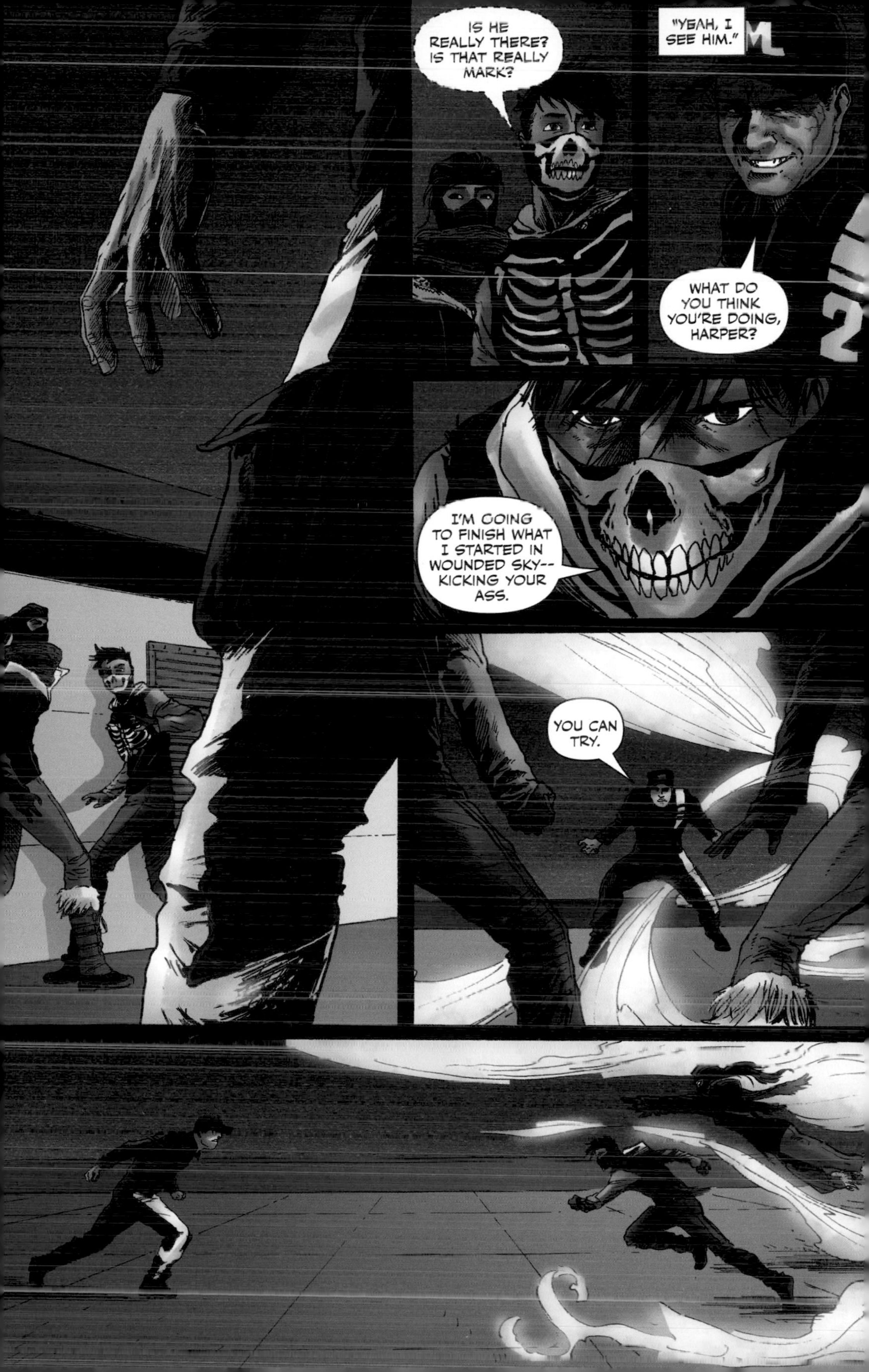
IS HE REALLY THERE? IS THAT REALLY MARK?
"YEAH, I SEE HIM."
WHAT DO YOU THINK YOU'RE DOING, HARPER?
I'M GOING TO FINISH WHAT I STARTED IN WOUNDED SKY-- KICKING YOUR ASS.
YOU CAN TRY.

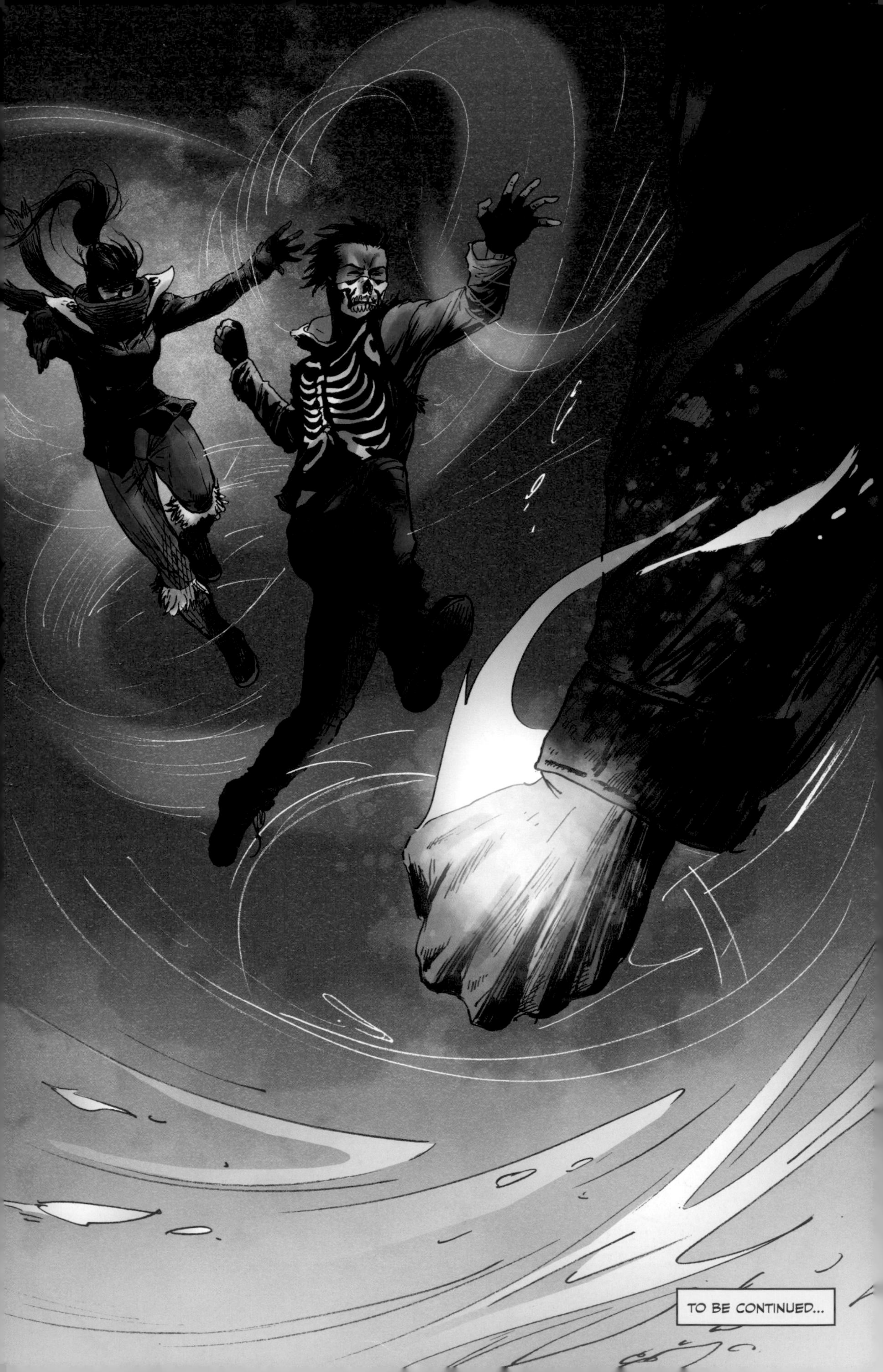
TO BE CONTINUED...

DAVID A. ROBERTSON (he, him, his) is an award-winning writer. His books include *When We Were Alone* (winner Governor General's Literary Award), *Will I See?* (winner Manuela Dias Book Design and Illustration Award), *Betty: The Helen Betty Osborne Story* (listed In The Margins), and the YA trilogy The Reckoner (winner Michael Van Rooy Award for Genre Fiction, McNally Robinson Best Book for Young People). David educates as well as entertains through his writings about Indigenous peoples in Canada, reflecting their cultures, histories, communities, as well as illuminating many contemporary issues. David is a member of Norway House Cree Nation. He lives in Winnipeg. | @DaveAlexRoberts